Just Desserts

A Perfect Dish Duo Novel

TAWDRA KANDLE

Just Desserts
Copyright © 2014 Tawdra Kandle

ISBN-978-1-68230-254-5

To my two sisters, Robyn and Kelly~
One by birth and blood
One by marriage and friendship
So much of both of you is in this story,
Especially Frank, Family and Food.
With much love always ...

PART
I

Ch♥pter One

"**WELL? WHAT DO you think?**"

I dragged my eyes from the Behavior Disorders text I'd been reading and glanced up at my roommate. She'd been changing her clothes since I got back from my last class, trying on one outfit after another.

"Ava, are you even looking?" I knew the hint of exasperation in Julia's voice covered up her nerves. I swallowed my impatience and studied her as she shifted from one foot to the other.

"Yes, of course I'm looking." I narrowed my eyes, taking in the jeans and gray sweater. "That looks nice."

Julia turned back toward the mirror. "I don't know. It's just not what I wanted. And the sweater itches."

"Then try something else. You don't want him to think you've got fleas or some weird body rash on your first date."

"Thanks." She disappeared into her closet again and came out with another hanger, this one bearing a pretty green scoop neck shirt. "Does the green look too much?"

I tilted my head, considering. "Too much what?"

"You know, too much ...like, too dressy for the movies."

I kept from rolling my eyes, but just barely. "It's a date, Jules. You want to look pretty. And that color really brings out your eyes. Besides, he's going to like you, whatever you wear. Go for it."

She didn't looked convinced, but she did stop talking as she stripped off the sweater and pulled the shirt over her head. It really was her color, and I smiled a little before I went back to my book. This date was a big deal: it was Julia's first time out with Jesse Fleming, the handsome son of her boss. They'd met while she was babysitting his little brother, and she was more excited than I'd seen her in a long time.

I managed to ignore Julia's mumbled debate with herself over shoes and actually got through two more pages before she planted herself in front of me again.

"Okay, I'm ready. How do I look?"

I marked my place again with my finger. "Breathtaking." I couldn't help grinning at the sparkle in her eyes. "Seriously, you look awesome. Is Jesse coming up here?"

"He's coming to the dorm, but I think I'll go down to meet him."

I arched an eyebrow. "Really? What, are you ashamed of me?" Ack, that was my mother's voice, coming right out of my mouth.

Julia laughed. "Of course not, silly. You can come down with me if you want. I just don't think he should have to brave the Friday night freshmen." She gave a mock shudder.

I sighed. Being a resident advisor to a floor full of emotional first-year college girls wasn't for the faint of heart. "Yeah, I get that. I think I'll pass on going down. If I go out there, someone who's having a crisis will find me and need nurturing. If I stay in here, there's a better chance the crisis will pass before she can track me down."

Julia snagged her coat off the back of her desk chair and shrugged into it. "Hope springs eternal." She took a deep breath and heaved it out. "Wish me luck."

I hopped off the bed and hugged her, the top of my head just about reaching her shoulders. "You don't need luck. Just relax and enjoy yourself." I stepped back, tamping down the unexpected flare of wistful envy that put a lump in my throat. "And text me at some point, so I know he hasn't taken you off into the woods to be his love slave."

Jules made a face at me as she turned the doorknob. "Please!" Whatever else she might have added was lost in her gasp of surprise when she swung the door open, revealing a tall familiar figure in the hallway.

Liam's hand was raised as though he had been about to knock. He looked as taken aback as Julia was.

"We need a peephole in this door so we don't open it to just anyone." She glanced at me over her shoulder, her eyes wide and pleading. I bit the corner of my lip, not sure what I could do to help. I didn't have experience with ex-boyfriends. Hell, I didn't have experience with boyfriends at all.

"Excuse me, I need to leave." Jules made to step around him. Liam didn't move.

"Where are you going?" He sounded more skeptical than curious, and I saw Julia's shoulders stiffen. Now he was just making her mad.

"Out." If he knew her at all, he would have just stood aside at that tone. But apparently nearly a year of dating hadn't given him a clue.

"Where?"

"None of your business." Julia craned her neck to

look down the hall, and I knew what she was thinking. The last thing she needed was for Jesse to come up and run into Liam. Talk about awkward.

"She has a date." I didn't mean to say it, but the words flew out of my mouth anyway. I stood with my arms folded over my chest as they both stared at me. After a minute, Jules took advantage of Liam's distraction and slipped past him.

"That's right. And I don't want to keep him waiting."

"Which one of your new men are you seeing tonight? Do you know what everyone is saying about you? Or don't you care?"

She stopped a few paces away but didn't turn around when she answered him.

"I thought I made it pretty clear this afternoon. I'm not your business any more, Liam. If I want to bang the whole football team, I will. So, good night, and don't let the door hit you in the ass on the way out."

"But I wanted to talk with you. This afternoon—"

"Should have told you everything you wanted to know. Leave me alone, Liam. Please."

I couldn't take it anymore. I moved forward to hold onto the door, leaning out so I could catch Julia's eye.

"How about this, Liam. You tell me what you have to say to Jules, and I'll decide if it's worth her time. If it is, you can talk to her later, when she's ready."

Julia smiled at me in gratitude, and I mouthed one word to her.

"Go."

She didn't need me to say it twice. Before Liam could speak again, Julia was down the hall, to the steps. I breathed a silent prayer that Jesse was waiting for her in the lobby.

"So who is he?" Liam stretched one arm to lean

against the door jam, his eyes fastened on me now. "Who's she seeing tonight?"

"No one you know. Really, Liam. Why are you here?"

He shifted his gaze away. "I told you. I'm worried about her. About what people are saying. Everyone's talking about Julia screwing around, sleeping with any guy who looks her way."

"You're going to want to shut the hell up. That's my best friend you're talking about. And you might remember she was also your girlfriend for ten months. What does that say about you?"

"Exactly. Do you know how my fraternity brothers are talking? It's sick. It makes me look bad, too."

"Oh, yeah? You mean like someone who dumps his girlfriend in front of all of their friends at the surprise birthday party she threw him?"

He had the grace to look away from me. "So it wasn't my finest hour. But like I told Julia, it was for the best. Even if she doesn't get that now, she will."

"Breaking up is one thing. Humiliation is another. She might get over it, but she'll never forgive you. And neither will I."

"I don't expect forgiveness from either of you. I just think she should rein it in, to stop slutting around campus. She needs to have a little self-respect."

Tomorrow morning, I was going to think of a killer comeback, but at the moment, anger closed my throat. I reached for the edge of the door to slam it in his face, but before I could do it, a group of freshmen girls appeared around the corner, giggling and talking in the high-pitched voices that went right up my spine.

Liam's face froze, and he stepped forward. "Ava, please. Let me come in. Just for a minute."

I frowned. "Are you crazy? No, you can't come in."

"Ava. *Please.*" His eyes darted back down the hallway, and I followed his gaze to one of the girls. Aha. Suddenly everything was clear.

I hesitated just long enough for Liam to sense weakness. He slid between the door and the wall, brushing against my body. Instinct made me shy back away from him. He pushed the door shut and leaned on it.

He was entirely too close to me, and I struggled to say something to get my balance back.

"Too many pissed-off girls, Liam? What's the matter? Your little freshman fuck-buddy giving you problems, too?"

He ran a hand through his light brown hair, scowling. "She wasn't my fuck-buddy. She was just ...convenient. And now she's a major pain in my ass."

His obvious discomfort made me feel better. I'd never seen the cool and aloof Liam Bailey in anything less than total control.

"What's she doing?"

Liam closed his eyes and shook his head. "Typical freshman shit. She just happens to show up outside my classes. Drunk texts me late at night. Has her friends talk to me in the dining hall." He pulled out Julia's chair and sat down.

"Make yourself at home, why don't you." I rolled my eyes, sinking onto my bed across from him and tucking my feet up beneath me.

"Sorry, but I'm not going back out there until the coast is clear. If she saw me come in here, she's probably walking back and forth down the hall, hoping to catch me leaving."

"Are you claiming sanctuary?" I couldn't help a little smile.

"Something like that." Liam's mouth tightened a little. "I didn't sleep with her, you know. With Rachel, the freshman. Not that night, not since. Not ever."

I raised one eyebrow, my skepticism clear.

"I didn't. The night of my birthday party, Giff walked her home after everyone left. And I haven't talked to her since. I mean, not to say more than, 'Go home, you're drunk. I'm not interested.'"

"If you weren't interested, why did you show up at your party—the party my best friend, your *girlfriend* worked long and hard planning, by the way—with your hand down the shirt of another woman?"

He shrugged. "The guys had a little pre-party for me at the Alpha Delt house. They'd invited some girls, and she was one of them. She was wasted before I even showed up. And she wouldn't leave me alone, kept saying she'd been watching me around campus and had a big crush on me. I don't know, one thing led to another and it seemed like it would be a way to make sure Julia knew I was moving on."

"Because just telling her, privately, and maybe with a little bit of sensitivity just wouldn't get the job done."

He sighed and sprawled back in the chair. "I never said it was the smart thing to do. If I could do it over, yeah, I probably would have made better choices. But there was more going on than you know. The whole thing is complicated."

I dropped to lie down on my side, bunching a pillow under my head. It didn't seem like Liam was planning to leave any time soon, so I decided to get comfortable. My textbook mocked me from the foot of the bed, and I ignored it.

"Complicated, huh? Care to elaborate?"

"Not really, no. Just take my word for it. But don't worry, I've felt like a dick since the morning after. And

7

even if I hadn't, Giff would've made sure I did. He was really pissed at me."

"Can you blame him? If you felt so bad, why didn't you apologize? Make it right with Julia?"

He closed his eyes and shook his head. "I told you, complicated. Plus, I figured it was done. Better let her just move on."

"And now that she has, in fact, moved on, suddenly you feel compelled to come back into her life?"

"Thanks, Dr. DiMartino. I didn't realize I was here for a session."

I grinned, unfazed. "You're stuck in a room with a psych major. You have two choices: leave and risk assault by freshman, or stay and answer my questions."

"I could stay and ignore you." Liam hooked one foot over the rung at the bottom of the chair.

"You could try."

He frowned, rubbed one hand over his forehead and blew out a breath. "Look, I don't want to talk about Julia. I know I screwed up with her. What's the point of rehashing the whole thing?"

I held his eye. "You tell me. You're the one who showed up here tonight, insisting on talking to her. You still haven't said why."

"No, I told you. The guys are talking about her. Everyone is calling her a slut."

"And you care ...why?"

"Because I feel responsible." The words came out as though he hadn't meant to say them. "Okay, is that what you wanted to hear? You know what Julia was like when we started going out. She was shy. Quiet. I was the first person she ..." His voice trailed off.

"I know." The flash of vulnerability on his face took away some of my mad.

"So if she's doing all of this, fucking around, because of what I did to her ...yeah, I feel like I have to say something."

I hesitated. I was right smack in the middle here: my best friend was looking for revenge on the guy who had screwed her over and humiliated her in a very public way. She wasn't actually sleeping with any of the guys Liam saw with her. It was all a giant con, a big set-up engineered by Julia, Liam's friend Giff and me, designed to make Liam want her back so she could shoot him down.

But there was no way I could tell Liam this, even if I wanted to. I wasn't going to break the sacred girlfriend code. Maybe he wasn't quite the jerk we thought—though I wasn't sure I bought it—but still, I couldn't forget who he was, and what he'd done.

"You may have been Julia's first serious boyfriend, Liam, but that doesn't mean you have to feel responsible. And ..." I licked my lips, trying to decide how to say what I wanted without giving away anything. "Come on. You know Jules. Does it seem like she'd start sleeping around, even if you did break her heart?"

He shook his head. "Yeah, I do know her. Or I thought I did. But what if she's, like, gone off the deep end? Some girls can't handle break-ups. They go nuts."

I couldn't help myself. I burst out laughing. "Wait a minute. So you're saying you think Julia's lost her mind because of what you did? Good God, Liam. Talk about arrogance."

I half-expected him to get defensive and maybe a little mad, but instead, he surprised me again by laughing, too.

"Yeah, I guess when I hear myself say it out loud, it sounds that way. Okay, so I didn't drive Julia to the edge of sanity by breaking up with her. So then why is she acting like this?"

"Maybe she's just enjoying her freedom." It wasn't even close to being true, but it sounded good. I decided a change of subject was in order. With one last longing glance at my book, I stood up. "Since it looks like you're going to be here for a little while, do you want a drink? I'm going to break out some wine coolers. I think we have some beer in the fridge, too."

"Sure, I'll have whatever you're drinking."

I dug out two of our high-class plastic cups, took two wine coolers from the fridge and poured us each a healthy portion.

"I can drink from the bottle," Liam offered.

"Better to hide it in a cup, in case Rachel the freshman or one of her buddies decides to come in." I tucked the empty and the extra behind my wastepaper basket.

"Gotcha." Liam held up his cup. "To ...friends, I guess."

I raised my eyebrows but touched my wine to his anyway. "Okay. If you say so."

He sipped and nodded. "Not bad. The wine cooler, I mean." He set it down on Julia's desk, carefully avoiding the mess of papers she'd left there. There was a moment of silence, but it wasn't uncomfortable.

"You know, I always enjoyed spending time with you." Liam traced a drop of moisture on the side of the cup. "Sometimes I felt like I could talk to you more than I could to Julia."

It felt disloyal to agree with him, but I nodded anyway. "I know what you mean. Jules said the same thing about Giff, actually. She misses him."

"Yeah. Too bad she isn't his type. They always got along better than Julia and me. If it weren't for Giff, we probably wouldn't have stayed together as long as we did."

This wasn't news to me. I'd seen the tension between my roommate and her boyfriend for months before the break-up had become official, but neither of them seemed to recognize it. If I'd said anything to Jules, she would have accused me of trying to psychoanalyze everything.

"Why did you? Stay together, I mean." I took another drink.

Liam lifted one shoulder. "I don't know. Why not? Julia is a nice person. She's pretty, she's smart ...my parents liked her. My dad kept saying she would make a good politician's wife."

"Julia? A political *wife?* That's crazy." I laughed and tilted my cup to catch the last drops. "I mean, seriously? You weren't thinking that far ahead, were you?"

Liam stared at me, an odd look on his face. "You should laugh more often. It makes your eyes sparkle."

I didn't know what to do with that. Liam paying me a compliment felt somehow wrong. "Don't change the subject. Were you seriously considering marrying Jules?"

He looked away from me. "I'm going to graduate next year. My future is pretty well mapped out, at least as far as my parents are concerned. And a girlfriend, who becomes a wife who can make me look good, is definitely on the list of things I need. According to the senator, anyway."

I reached for one of the bottles and poured myself a refill, holding it to Liam in question. He hesitated a minute and then took it from me, adding to what was still in his cup.

"I'm sorry, is this 1954? And is your last name Kennedy? Who thinks that way anymore?" The booze warmed me and loosened my tongue.

"Yeah, I know. But it's my dad's dream. His father only got to county politics, but Dad made it to Congress.

And maybe he'll go further. But he's counting on me to take it all the way to the big time."

"Do you want to do it?" I finished my second glass and curled on my side again, looking up at Liam.

He met my eyes, and something flashed there. Defiance or pain, I couldn't tell which. He didn't answer me at first. Instead he tossed back the last of his cooler and took another refill.

"Here, why don't you kill it?" Without waiting for me to answer, he poured the rest into my cup. I rarely had more than two drinks, even if we were just staying in the room, but I couldn't think of a good reason not to right now.

"Nice dodge and re-direct, but you didn't answer me. Do you even want to go into politics?"

"I don't know." He spoke low, his eyes on the floor. "I thought I did. I mean, I'm good at it. My parents have been training me as long as I can remember. I never thought about doing anything else."

"So what changed?" I maneuvered the cup to my lips and managed to sip without shifting.

"Nothing. Or maybe everything. Maybe me."

This Liam Bailey was not the same smooth, confident guy I'd known for the last year. He seemed troubled, almost sad. Or maybe that was just the three cups of wine talking.

"Well, guess what? The good news for you is that you're only a junior in college. You have time. You're a history and poli sci major, and that can translate into something other than running for office. Or you could change your major, though it's a little late in the game for that. Or you could—"

"Or I could do this." Before I could move or react, Liam slid off the chair onto his knees and leaned over me, covering my lips with his.

At first, I was stunned into complete paralysis. *Liam Bailey was kissing me.* Me, Ava DiMartino, the dumpy little Italian girl. The one who didn't do dates, who had a plan and goals and no time for boys.

And then he moved his hand to the side of my face, and his tongue traced the seam of my mouth. A moan caught in my throat, and I opened my lips, kissing him back for a wild minute of insanity. Liam slid his free arm under my back. The wall of his chest teased against the tips of my breasts, and he lifted his head to trail kisses across my face and murmur into my ear.

"My God, Ava, you feel amazing. And you smell like ..." Nose buried in my neck, he inhaled deeply. "Lilacs. Like my grandmother's garden in spring." His hand covered my breast.

Something within me snapped, jerking me back to reality, cutting through the wine-haze. I pushed against his shoulders.

"Liam, stop. Move. We can't do this. What's wrong with you?"

He leaned up, frowning down into my face. "Why? What?"

"Holy—you need to get up. God, what was I thinking?" I kicked at his leg. "Get the hell off me." I squirmed, trying to get away from the heat of his body. "Clearly I wasn't thinking at all. It's the alcohol. Wine is bad. Wine coolers, I mean. So, so bad."

"I hope you were thinking that you liked me kissing you." He lowered his face toward me again, and without thinking about it, I hauled off and smacked him.

"What the *hell*—" He jumped to his feet, holding his jaw. "What did you do that for?"

I scooted up to sit near my pillows. "Be happy that

was all I did. I'm Italian. You're lucky I didn't rip your balls off."

Liam climbed onto the foot of the bed, avoiding me with care, and leaned against the wall. His face was flushed, especially where I'd hit him, and his light brown hair, usually in such artful disarray, was looking decidedly rumpled. He dropped his head back, and it thumped against the wall.

"I don't get why it's so bad." He spoke with his eyes closed.

I eyed his long, lean body, trying to ignore the evidence of desire that stretched the zipper of his jeans. Swallowing hard, I focused on his feet. Black Converse. Totally unsexy. Except they weren't. Okay, so no focusing on any of his body parts. What in the hell was wrong with me?

"How can you not get it?" I gritted my teeth and curled my legs up, wrapping my arms around them until I was huddled in a ball. I let my hair drop around my face, giving the illusion of protection. "Whatever else might have been screwed up with you, I always thought you had a logical brain. Point A: Julia is my best friend and my roommate. Point B: She was your girlfriend for nearly a year—"

"Ten months." Liam didn't move as he mumbled.

I pushed my hair back and peeked out at him. "See, that is such a guy thing. Ten months *is* nearly a year. What I'm saying is, it's not like you just went out once or twice. You were together. Like, together, together. So it is not cool at all for you to kiss me. It violates every rule in the girl code."

"Maybe I'm out of practice, but it sure felt like you were kissing me back." He opened his eyes and turned his head to look at me, the smolder in his gaze making it hard for me to sit still. Even though most of me was flooded with guilt, another part was telling me to leap down the bed and climb into his lap. The image made me groan.

"Stop looking at me like that. Okay, yes, I was kissing you back. But I was wrong. I'm a terrible person. I'm probably going to hell now. At the very least, I'm looking at extra time in purgatory. My mother is going to have to light so many candles for me."

A slow smile spread across Liam's face as he dropped to his hands and knees and began crawling toward me. He reminded me of a mountain lion, and the look in his eyes was definitely predatory.

"Well, if you're already damned, you might as well have some fun, right?" He grabbed one of my feet and yanked down, pulling me flat again. I kicked at him, missing his shoulder as he dodged. He planted one hand on either side of my hips and dropped to kiss my neck, running his lips down to my collarbone.

"Liam." I pushed at his head. "Stop." My words were weak, probably because him stopping was really not what I wanted. It was what I *should* want. But he complied anyway, rising up again so he could look at me.

"I know what you're saying. Yeah, it's kind of weird, I guess. But not really. I always liked you. What I said before was true. I thought we got along pretty well, and God, Ava, if Julia is moving on, why shouldn't we?"

"Oh, so if you walked in on Giff and Julia in bed together, you'd be okay with that?"

He smirked. "I'd be shocked. Ava, I hate to break it to you, but Giff is gay."

I swatted his arm. "It's the principle of it, and you know what I mean. And not only that, but I'm not looking to get tangled up with you or with anyone. I don't have time for this."

"Can you tell me honestly you don't feel this spark?" He moved to lie alongside me and skimmed a hand down my side, from my hip to the side of my breast. "You weren't pushing me away a few minutes ago."

I heaved out a breath. "Just because I feel something doesn't mean I have to act on it. I don't have any interest in being your fuck buddy tonight, Liam. Spark or no spark."

"I'm not looking for that either. Didn't you hear what I said? I like you, Ava. I always have. Kissing you might not have been what I planned to do tonight, but this isn't the first time I've thought of doing it."

I squirmed as he ran a finger up my bare arm. "Oh, really? So you're saying you thought about this when you were going out with my best friend? Because that doesn't make you look any better."

He fell back on the bed, hard. I could still feel his warmth all along one side of me.

"Remember I said that my reasons for breaking up with Julia were complicated?"

"Yeah ..." I frowned as the meaning of his words dawned on me. "You're saying I was the reason you did it? Oh, come on, Liam. What kind of idiot do you think I am?"

"I don't think you're an idiot at all, and what the hell does that mean?"

I held up one hand and began counting on my fingers. "One, you're trying to say that you broke up with Julia because you had feelings for me? If you expect me to believe that, you really must think I'm stupid. Or desperate. I'm neither. Two, if I were to believe that, you feel it should be enough to make me want to fall into your arms here and now? If that's the case, you must think I'm not only dumb but really shallow, too."

"I didn't. And I don't. The complications are lot more—uh, complicated than just me liking you. But it played into it. You can believe me or not, but by last fall, I started to realize that the only time I really enjoyed hanging out with Julia was when you were there, too. So I knew it was time to end things, before I did something really stupid like get drunk and try to make out with you while I was still dating your friend."

I snorted. "Like that would have ever happened."

Liam shook his head. "Yeah, I know, but I wanted to. And that was enough. So no, it wasn't the only reason, but it was a factor. I didn't come here tonight to tell you that, or to do ...this ..." He turned over again so he was looking down at me, and he touched the side of my face with the tip of his finger. "But I'm not sorry it happened, and I'm not sorry it's out there. And I don't think we did anything wrong."

I held still, hardly breathing. I was afraid if I moved, I might not be able to control my hands. Or my lips. Good God, when did this happen? When did I stop hating Liam Bailey? Or maybe I still did, but maybe hating him didn't necessarily preclude wanting to rub my body all over his ...

I rolled away from him. "That's the difference between us, isn't it? I know what we did was wrong, because it's not something I'd be comfortable telling Jules. Plus, I think you're just saying what you did to make yourself feel better. I don't know what kind of game you're playing, but I'm not going to be part of it. Just go away."

Liam sighed, and for a minute, he didn't move. Then he threw one leg over me, and for one dizzying breath, I thought he was going to kiss me again. But instead, he perched on the edge of the bed and dropped his head into his hands.

"I can't blame you for not trusting me, Ava. I know I haven't given you any reason to believe me. But I'm going to. I'm going to do whatever it takes to make you see that I'm not that guy. I want a chance with you."

I kept my eyes trained on the wall across the room. "Don't bother, because I'm not interested. I don't have time for games, and I'm not looking for a booty call."

He stood. "I'm not, either. No offense, but if that's what I wanted, there's plenty of willing girls." He pointed at the door. "I could just call Rachel the freshman, right? But I don't. I didn't mean to act on this yet, but I'm not sorry you know."

Liam snagged his coat from the chair, picked up his empty plastic cup and chucked it into the trash.

"Thanks for the wine. And the sanctuary. I'll talk to you soon."

He opened the door and disappeared into the now-quiet hallway. I heard the click of the lock as the door shut.

I should have been mad. Pissed and outraged and full of righteous indignation. But instead, a tiny seed of something unexpected and unfamiliar took root within me. I hugged my pillow to my chest for a few minutes, staring up at the ceiling.

When I reached to the end of the bed for my psych text, it no longer held the same appeal as it had a few hours before. I closed the book, slid it onto my desk and climbed under the covers. It was the first time I'd gone to bed without finishing my reading in a very long time.

That lasted about five minutes before I jumped up, turned the light back on and grabbed my book.

Ch♥pter Two

POUNDING ECHOED THROUGH the room and reverberated within my head. I groaned, wrapping my pillow over my ears and wishing for someone to make it the noise go away.

"Jules, it's someone at the door. Make them stop."

Julia swore under her breath as she dragged herself across the room to open the door. Through a blue haze of sleep, I heard her having a conversation. Was that Giff? Or was this some kind of weird dream?

I scented coffee and donuts, moaned and grumbled under my breath. "For the love of everything holy, shut the hell up."

I tried to climb back into oblivion. Julia had come home the night before just before I finally finished my homework. She was practically floating, and I hid my own guilt over Liam and our illicit make-out session by letting her ramble on about the movie, dimples and first kisses. She talked for a long time, and we hadn't gone to sleep until after two.

The door closed finally, leaving behind blessed silence. I lifted my head. "Quick, lock it before anyone else comes in. Good God, have people never heard of Saturdays? The morning when you don't wake up your friends?"

Julia didn't answer, but I heard her fumbling in the box of donuts and got a whiff of chocolate as she passed my bed on the way back to her own.

I snuggled back beneath the comforter and let sleep wash over me again until I heard the bathroom door open. A wave of steam hit me. I kept my face deep in the pillow.

"Was Giff really here this morning, or did I have a very detailed nightmare?"

Julia leaned over to dry her hair with the towel. "He was here. Good news is he brought coffee and donuts. Bad news is he set me up with someone else in the on-going plan to make Liam jealous."

A stab of something I didn't quite recognize shot through me. Dread or disappointment? I wasn't ready to examine it yet. I rolled over and pushed to sit up, punching my pillows behind me.

"Was there something about wrestling? I thought that had to be a dream."

She made a face as she reached for the comb. "It wasn't, sadly. I'm going to a meet this morning."

I leaned over my desk, where the foam coffee cup Giff had left was still waiting for me. "Oh, Jules." My brothers had wrestled, and I'd sat through more than my share of monotonous meets. I didn't envy my roommate having to go on this so-called date. Taking a sip of the coffee, I made a face. "Hey, this is cold. Can you zap it for me?"

Julia paused to glance at me in mid-tug as she pulled on her jeans. "Yeah, just a second." She buttoned her pants and reached for my cup. I watched her pour the coffee into my "Italian Princess" mug, stick it into the microwave and hit a button. Guilt made me offer the ultimate sacrifice.

"Do you want me to come with you?" I tried to look as though I meant it.

Julia laughed. "No, I'm not that mean. But I was thinking after Giff left. I'm putting my foot down. This is it. I'm done. Liam isn't jealous about me hanging out with guys. You said last night he only wanted to warn me about what people are saying, right? Because he feels guilty?"

The memory of Liam's face as he lowered his lips to mine brought a rush of both warmth and pain. The microwave beeped, and I jumped out of bed. I couldn't meet Julia's eyes as I tested the coffee again.

"Ava?" Her voice was tentative as she stretched a red Henley over her head. "Are you okay?"

"Of course." I stretched my lips into what I hoped looked like a smile. "Why wouldn't I be?"

She frowned. "I don't know, you got a funny look on your face. Did Liam say something else last night? When I got home, your eyes almost looked like you'd been crying. You can tell me if Liam was a jerk. I really don't care. I mean, unless he was a jerk to you."

A jerk? I paused, considering. "No, I told you everything." *Well, not everything.* "He was trying to find out why you're slutting it up, but he says it's just because he doesn't want you getting hurt. I asked him why it mattered to him, when he hadn't done a very good job of not hurting you himself. He said he felt like it would be his fault if you were doing it just to get back at him."

Julia's face pinked. "I'd have to say his ego was a little inflated if he wasn't actually on to us. So he's not interested in me because I'm unattainable again, he's worried that my broken heart is making me a little too obtainable. To other guys, at least. Lovely."

I swallowed over a lump in my throat. In the three years I'd known her, I'd never kept a genuine secret from Julia. It felt wrong. I turned my back, sipping the coffee and burning my tongue.

"Where are the donuts?"

"Over on my desk. Seriously, Ave, are you okay? You look ...weird."

"I'm fine." I opened the box and scouted for a glazed. "I'm just a little tired still. I think I'll crawl back under the covers and go to sleep for a while." I found a napkin and took my donut back to bed.

"All right, if you're sure."

I nibbled at the pastry for a few minutes before I gave up trying to swallow it and balled it into the napkin. Julia was drying her hair, and I took advantage of her preoccupation and slid back down under the covers. Closing my eyes, I willed myself into a troubled sleep.

I TOSSED AND turned for about forty-five minutes after Julia left. I vacillated between kicking myself for not telling her the truth and trying to convince myself that what had happened between Liam and me wasn't that big a deal.

Finally I sat up in bed and tossed off the blankets. I wasn't accomplishing anything just laying here. I had paperwork to do for the RA meeting this week, and there was always more reading to do for classes. Plus there was laundry, and I needed to call my mother and do my weekly check-in before she assumed I was dead and sent my brothers out after me.

Thinking of just that scenario, I reached for my phone,

unplugging it from the charger. I had put it on silent early last night, since I had stayed in all evening. My freshman girls knew all too well how to find me in my room.

I was surprised to see I had three missed calls and four text messages. Frowning, I turned the phone on and checked the calls first. All three were from an unfamiliar number, and there was one voice mail.

The texts were from the same number, and when I read them, my mouth dropped open.

Ava, call me back. I need to talk to you.

This is Liam. And I want you to call me. Please.

If you don't call me back, I'm coming over there now.

Okay, I won't come over, but call me as soon as you can.

I checked the times on the messages. The first two had been sent last night, and then two more had come this morning. I was almost afraid to listen to his voice mail. But I was a glutton for punishment, so I hit the button.

Ava, it's Liam. I just got back to my room. I want to talk to you about what happened. Call me back. Or have breakfast with me in the morning. We can go off-campus so no one recognizes us, but I want to see you again.

No good-bye, no nothing. Just a click. I frowned down at my phone, staring at the number for a moment before I hit the delete key.

In the clear, cold light of day, I could think rationally. Liam and I had both had been drinking. We were talking about things that were emotionally charged. That was it.

There wasn't any more to the kissing than that, which was probably why he wanted to talk to me so badly. Once he got back to his dorm, he'd realized the truth and wanted to make sure I didn't tell anyone he'd been making out with someone like me.

Or, if I bought into the theory that Liam was as diabolical as Jules thought, he had set out to hurt her again on purpose, and I'd fallen into the trap. Stupid, stupid wine.

I swiped my phone live again and replied to his last text.

I'm not calling you. Last night didn't mean anything, and don't worry, I won't tell anyone.

I hit send and tossed my phone onto the bed. Enough of this. It was time to forget about those few crazy minutes and get on with my Saturday. I found a pair of sweats and an old t-shirt in the bottom dresser drawer and was just heading toward the bathroom when I heard a knock at the door.

For one flash of time, I thought it might be Liam. He'd gotten my text but had come over anyway. I ran a hand over my hair, which was total bed-head, sticking up in every direction. Good grief, I was a mess.

"Ava, are you up?" The voice on the other side of the door was decidedly feminine. One of my freshman, and dammit, there was the tremble of tears behind her words. This wasn't going to be a simple hey-can-I-borrow-some-shoes visit. This was I-got-my-heart-broke counseling. I was so not in the mood.

Taking a deep breath, I swung open the door and barely bit back a groan. *Great.* Rachel, Liam's needy freshman, was leaning against the wall, her eyes watery and her nose red.

"Hi, Rachel." I tried to keep derision out of my voice.

24

"What do you need? Do you have a cold?" *Please have a cold.*

"No, I just wanted ...to talk to you." She sniffled and wiped at her face with a wadded-up tissue. "The other girls said you're pretty cool about giving advice."

I stretched my mouth into a smile. "Okay, so what can I do for you?"

She pointed over my shoulder into the room. "Can I come in? It's kind of private."

Those words struck terror in the heart of any resident advisor. "Sure." I stood back and let her in. "Sorry, I just got up, so things are kind of a mess."

She dropped onto Julia's bed without invitation, and I winced, thinking of how much my roommate would not appreciate this.

"I know it's kind of early, and I'm sorry for bothering you like this." She fumbled with the tissue, trying to find a dry spot. I grabbed my own box of Kleenex and offered it to her.

"Thanks." She blew her nose loudly and chucked the crumpled ball into the trash can. "So anyway, I just don't know what to do. And I think my friends are tired of me talking about it to them. They told me I should come see you. I was thinking about it, and then last night ..." Her voice trailed off, and her eyes welled again.

I closed my eyes and gritted my teeth. Damn Liam Bailey and the girls he led on. Dealing with his weeping cast-offs seemed to be my destiny in life.

"Last night?" I prompted her. I wasn't sure what she had seen.

She drew in a long, shaky breath. "I saw Liam Bailey going into your room. I know he used to date your room-mate, and I ..." Her face turned red. "I know what she must think of me. I mean, I didn't know what was hap-

25

pening that night. I just started talking to him at the Alpha Delt house, and then I was, um ..." Her eyes slid sideways. She was smart enough to know that she shouldn't tell her RA that she'd been indulging in underage drinking.

"Yeah, I can imagine." I didn't need the paperwork that came with that admission. "Listen, Rachel, you don't need to tell me all this."

"But I do." She leaned forward, her watery blue eyes wide and full of freshman earnestness. "Because I know what you must think of me. Like I'm some slut or something. But I'm not. Nothing happened with us. He took me with him to the party, and then after ...all that bad stuff, his roommate walked me home and told me not to expect to hear from Liam ever again."

Well, that jived with what Liam had said to me the night before. I worked hard to keep my face impassive yet compassionate.

"Okay, Rachel, so what can I do for you today? If you're worried that I think less of you because of that night, please don't. I know what goes down with freshman girls and upperclassmen. I'm sorry it happened to you, but you're not the first, and you won't be the last. Julia isn't mad at you either." Mentally I crossed my fingers that this would solve her problem and get her out of my room, even though I knew deep inside I was doomed to disappointment.

"That's really nice of you. Both of you. But that's not why I'm here. See, even though his roommate told me Liam wouldn't call me, I kept thinking he would. He might. I'm pretty sure he really liked me, and maybe he's just waiting a little while until his old girlfriend—well, you know. Gets over him. But I heard she's been with lots of other guys now, and I thought he was ready. I've tried to talk to him, but it's always in a crowd, so I guess he doesn't want to say anything until we're alone. But then I saw him here last night. I didn't know you guys were friends."

"What?" I was so lost in her convoluted train of thought that for a minute, I didn't catch the last part. "Friends? No, not really. We know each other."

"Then maybe you could say something to him about me. Maybe even set something up for us. You know, like, some place private. You could tell him I still like him."

I bit back a snort. "Rachel, I'm going to be straight with you, because I get the feeling that brutal honesty is the only thing you're going to understand. I'm sorry about it, but it's better that you know the truth. Liam is not interested in you. At all. He was here last night to talk to Julia, and he ducked into our room when he saw you in the hallway because he didn't want to run into you. Not in public, definitely not in private. I know that hurts. But it's better that you hear me now, believe me, and get over him than you make a fool out of yourself, chasing a boy who's embarrassed by you. Do you understand?"

Her big eyes blinked, and for a minute, she didn't move. And then her lip trembled a little and the tears spilled down her cheeks.

"Noooo ..." She was full-out wailing, and panic clutched me.

"C'mon, don't do that." I patted her shoulder, glancing at the door. "This isn't as bad as you think. Just move on, forget him—try to get to know some guys in your own class. And remember it's not you, it's him. Liam Bailey really is kind of a dick."

"But are you sure?" She was in the heaving-sobs portion of her meltdown. "I told all my friends we were going out. That he was just waiting for things to settle down. Oh my God, they're going to think I'm such an idiot."

27

"If they're really your friends, they'll understand. But you should talk to them. Tell them what a jerk Liam is, and I promise you, they'll have your back." I stood up, hoping she'd get the hint that our therapy session was now over.

"Okay." Rachel rose, too, and grabbing more tissues, she moved toward the door. "But if something changes ...if he tells you he's interested ...will you—"

"He's not going to. And nothing is going to change. Go have fun with some decent guys. And your friends. Friends don't let you down."

She nodded again, and with one last face-mopping and shuddering breath, she was gone. Out the door, in the hallway, and no longer my problem. For now, at least.

I dropped back onto my bed, closing my eyes as guilt rode me. *Friends don't let you down.* Only I did. A flash memory of lying here on this bed, with Liam over me, burned my mind, and I groaned, burying my face in the pillow. I was a horrible person. I had betrayed my best friend with the guy who had made her life hell. And what was worse, I couldn't say for certain that I wouldn't do the same thing again if he were here.

I rolled off the bed and reached for my Behavior Disorders notebook. I had an outline due for my term paper in that class this week, and it still needed a little work. And then there was a quiz coming up in Cognitive Psych. I wasn't too worried about it, but still, no need to take chances. I flipped open my dinosaur of a laptop and found the files I needed. For a peaceful thirty minutes, nothing existed for me outside of the work. This was my safe place, where everything was controlled and in order. No confusing feelings, no guilt, regrets or yearning. Only facts and theories were my dependable friends.

The door flew open, startling me out of the study zone. Julia stomped in, her cheeks red from the cold and her eyes stormy.

"Hey ..." I began, and then my stomach clenched. *Liam had told her. She knew. Oh, my God.* I swallowed and tried again to speak. "What's wrong?"

Jules ripped off her coat and tossed it in the general direction of the line of hooks behind the door. Not surprisingly, it missed, but she ignored it as she swung around to look at me.

"Liam Bailey is what's wrong. He's very, very wrong."

Shit. I licked my lips and tried to think of the right thing to say. Anything that would explain why I had made out with her ex-boyfriend last night. But maybe she didn't know. I decided to hedge first.

"So I take it he was there? At the meet?"

"Yes." Julia sat on the edge of her bed, stretching her legs out in front of her until her shoe almost hit one of my piles of papers. I moved it back out of the way. "I spent over an hour learning more about wrestling than I ever wanted to know. And then when I finally escaped, made it outside, *he* was there. Waiting for me. Turns out he's come up with a really great idea. A selfless plan designed to help me out. He's willing to sleep with me, just out of the goodness of his heart. Isn't that big of him?"

My heart pounded, and all at once even that bite of doughnut I'd eaten felt like a bad decision. "He *what?*"

"Yep, you heard me right. Sex without any of the annoying strings attached. That's what he's offering me." She clutched the sheet in both fists and pulled up. "I just want to scream. I haven't been this mad since right after his birthday party."

My mind was whirling. *He'd used me.* Here I was mooning around about what Liam had said last night, about his texts and calls, and it had all been part of his nasty little game. I was stupid.

I laced my hands together, just to keep from falling apart. "I don't blame you. That's just horrible."

Jules dropped onto her back, staring up at the ceiling. "You know, the sad part is that I had started to second-guess everything. I was planning to back off the whole revenge plan. Not now. Now, I'm upping the ante."

Dread tensed my shoulders. "What you going to do?"

"No more messing around with Giff's plans. I'm going to tell him what his precious best friend said to me. And then I'm going to write out the whole sordid story, from the time he asked me out, all about the birthday party and then about today's mess. And I'm naming names, and it's going up on the blog."

It felt wrong. As a matter of fact, this whole deal, getting even with Liam, suddenly looked petty and immature, like a frat house the morning after a wild party. Julia and her project partner had started a blog to share the stories of girls—and guys—who'd been done wrong by their exes. It had turned into a positive exercise, but using it to slam Liam would change all of that.

"Jules, are you sure? Is that going to solve anything? And what about Jesse?"

She rolled over to face me, and I saw regret in her expression. "I know. I thought about him right away. But, God, Ave, Liam deserves some kind of payback for everything he's done to me. This is totally separate from Jesse and me."

She was delusional, I thought. Anger and hurt were blurring her vision. "Can you keep it that way? Don't you think he's going to find out, and be pissed? I know you've only had one date, but it seems like there's potential for a lot more. You don't want to screw that up."

Julia blew her hair out of her face, frowning. "I'll

burn that bridge when I get to it."

Ch♥pter Three

I BURIED MYSELF in books, papers and studying for the rest of the weekend. Julia didn't argue when I suggested take-out for dinner Saturday night; I didn't want to take a chance on running into Liam anywhere on campus. We had a movie marathon while we both did homework, and my favorite chick flicks took my mind off all the distractions.

I sent Jules on a candy run before we started up *The Ugly Truth*. My stomach had finally settled, thanks to the dependability of reading assignments and lecture notes, and I was craving peanut butter cups. She'd only been gone about ten minutes when my phone buzzed. I reached for it without looking, thinking she needed candy buying guidance.

But no. It was a text message from Liam, and all that peace I'd been skirting around disappeared.

Ava, can you talk?

I sat looking at the words for a minute and then hit delete. I switched the ringer to vibrate and turned the phone to face the floor so I couldn't see the screen. I had just picked up my pen again when I heard the vibration. *Damn technology.*

Determined to ignore it, I focused on the notes in front of me for a full three minutes. And then I flipped the phone over.

I need to see you. I'll meet you somewhere. Or I can come over there.

My eyes widened, and my fingers flew across the keyboard.

No! Don't come over. I don't want to see you. Or talk to you.

He must have been waiting for me to reply, because only seconds after I hit send, another message popped up.

Will you have dinner with me tomorrow night?

I gritted my teeth. I didn't know how much clearer I could be.

No. And stop texting me.

I held the phone for a few minutes, waiting, but there were no more messages. I breathed a deep sigh—I told myself it was of relief, but I'd be lying if I didn't admit to a pang of disappointment—and went back to my notebook.

The phone vibrated again, this time longer, moving it across the little area rug I kept next to my bed. Not a text this time; now he was calling me.

I kept my eyes glued to the words on the paper, even though they meant nothing to me at the moment. Long minutes after the buzzing stopped, there was one more gasp of an alert. Voice mail, of course.

Hitting delete without listening would have been the

smart choice, but clearly I was losing my mind. I hit play and watched the door the whole time, anticipating Julia coming back with my candy. As soon as I heard his voice, I could tell he was drunk. There was a music and laughter in the background, and his words slurred.

Ava. It's me. Liam. Listen, I just want to see you. Please let me explain in person. I promise it's not what you think. But I want—shit, I don't want to talk to your voice mail. Call me back.

The recording went on a little longer, though Liam didn't say anything else. I heard voices, muffled now. He had probably forgotten to hit end and put the phone back in his pocket. I deleted the message and wished I had never heard of Liam Bailey. He hadn't planned to kiss me. Was that supposed to make me feel better? What was I, convenient? And why the hell did that thought sting so much?

Julia came back and dumped a load of chocolate in my lap, chattering away as she took off her jacket. I shoved my telephone up onto my bed, under the pillow, where I wouldn't be able to hear the vibration buzzing.

Tearing open the wrapper on a candy bar, I hit play on the remote. Gerard Butler was definitely one of my favorite actors, but in this movie, he reminded me a little too much of someone I wanted to forget.

I pointed at the screen. "Ever notice Gerard is a little bit of jerk in this one?"

Julia laughed as she drew a blanket over her lap. "Honey, I have it on good authority that they're all dicks."

Truer words never spoken, I thought, and took another big bite of chocolate.

LIAM CONTINUED TO send texts and call me for the next two days. I didn't answer anything; I deleted each message and wondered about the feasibility of changing my phone number. Having to explain to Julia why I was doing it would be a problem.

It rattled me, though. I couldn't concentrate on studying, and I had trouble sleeping. The cognitive psych quiz, which should have been a breeze, looked like it was written in Greek as I struggled through it.

It snowed Monday night, and that only added more complications to my life. I was late to my clinical after having to shovel out the car, and I barely got to my next class on time. The professor droned on as I tried to concentrate and ignore my wet feet. Right before dismissing us, he handed back the quizzes from the day before. My heart sank when I saw a C in red at the top of my paper.

The rest of the students began talking as they stood, packing up bags to leave. I moved slower, carefully replacing everything in my notebook and sliding it into my backpack, as though it mattered. I couldn't remember the last time I'd gotten anything below an A on a test. An occasional B on a paper, yes, because those were subjective, but if it were just a strict regurgitation of information, or even analysis of theories, I was on top of it.

I couldn't afford to get C's. I was only here by the grace of scholarships and my job as resident advisor at the dorm. The idea of losing all that now just because some stupid boy had taken away my focus—that was unthinkable.

The professor was still in the front, typing into his computer. I slung my backpack over my shoulder as I approached him.

He looked up and smiled. "Ms. DiMartino. What can

I do for you?"

I licked my lip. "That quiz—I'm sorry. I did study for it, and I thought I knew the information. I don't know what happened."

He shook his head. "What do you mean? What happened?"

"I got a C."

"Oh. Right. Well, it was one of the tougher ones. No one aced it."

I raised my eyebrows. "What can I do to make up for it? Can I write an extra paper? Or re-take it?"

Frowning, he shook his head. "It's just a quiz. Don't let it bother you. Your average in this class is almost perfect, if I remember right. One C isn't going to fail you."

I drew in a shaky breath. "I don't want it to bring down my GPA. I'm here on an academic scholarship."

He laughed. "Oh, Ms. DiMartino, if only my other students had just a little of your academic passion. But don't let it give you an ulcer. Maybe you've been working too hard, and you need to give yourself a break."

"I don't take breaks." That kind of thinking was what let people veer off-course and led to bad things. Things I didn't want to think about.

He shook his head. "Well, try not to stress, okay? If you're having trouble with the material, my door is always open. But I think you're overreacting about this grade. You're doing fine."

The professor closed the computer and slid it into the case, which I knew meant this talk was over. I buttoned my coat as I opened the door to the cold gray of the late afternoon.

"Ava."

Liam's voice broke through my preoccupation. I stopped without turning around as annoyance flared.

"Not a good time." I spoke though clenched teeth. "What are you doing here?"

"Waiting for you. I know all the psych classes are in this building, so I figured you'd probably be here sooner or later. I've been sitting out here for the last forty-five minutes."

Part of me wanted to smile. *He'd been waiting for me that long, on the off-chance I might be in this building?* Then I remembered the quiz, and I steeled myself.

"That's a little creepy, Liam. Taking up stalking?" I kept my back to him, afraid meeting his eyes would weaken my resolve.

"I wouldn't have to stalk you if you answered my texts or phone calls."

I wheeled around, my eyes wide, and tilted my head in pretended surprise. "Hmm ...not picking up your calls or answering your texts ...you almost might think I didn't want to talk to you."

Looking at him was a mistake. He was leaning against a column, his hands deep in the pockets of the tan jacket that was buttoned high on his neck. His brown hair ruffled in the wind, and his eyes were stormy as he stared down at me. My traitorous hands wanted to run through his hair and smooth it down.

I bit down hard on that thought. Standing in front of me was the reason I'd been miserable all weekend, the cause of my disastrous quiz grade, and the person who'd offered my best friend strings-free sex just hours after kissing me senseless. There would be no touching.

He pushed off the column and stood closer to me. My heart skipped a little, but I willed myself not to take a step backward.

I pushed past him, intent on walking away.

"What the hell, Ava? I just want to talk with you."

I snorted. "Well, I don't want to talk to you. Or even see you. I want you to go away and leave me alone."

"Can we please just go some place and talk? It's cold out here. And I'm not going to give up. If you won't come with me, I'll just show up at your room. Your choice."

I glanced around. There were still a number of students meandering in and out of the building, and a few girls cast curious looks our way. Liam didn't maintain a low profile. He was a track star, son of a local political celebrity and active with Alpha Delt. I didn't know many females who wouldn't love to date him; even just standing here talking to him could start talk.

"Fine. But not any place someone might see us. And not for long. I'm busy."

Liam smiled, and I averted my eyes. I couldn't show weakness.

He pointed to the brick path that led behind the building. "My car's in B lot, right here. Did you walk or drive?"

"I had to park back at the dorm. They hadn't plowed enough for me to get a spot here after clinical."

"I'll drive you home, then. Come on." He turned and headed down the hill, leaving me to follow, thinking what a bad idea this whole thing was.

I didn't have trouble finding his black BMW, shiny against the snow banks. He clicked it unlocked and opened the passenger side door for me, and then jogged around to his side. Once in, he turned the key, cranked up the heat and flipped a switch near the gear shift.

"Heated seats. You'll be toasty in a minute."

I raised my eyebrows. "Nice. Us peasants are just happy when the heater blows hot air."

Liam ignored me as he backed out, one hand on the headrest of my seat. "How about we get some coffee on our way to the dorm?"

"Oh, that's a great idea. Let's go to Beans, the place I hang out with my friends, and sit down there to talk. I'm sure no one will notice us."

He sighed. "Give me some credit, okay? I thought I could run in, grab us some coffees to go, and then we could drink them in the car. I just spent a long time out in the cold. I could use something hot." He shot me a look under a quirked eyebrow. "Unless you'd like to warm me up in another way. I'd give up coffee for that."

My face heated. "God, Liam. Fine. Go get your coffee. Just park in the back, please. Your car isn't exactly inconspicuous."

He drove off campus into Gatbury, the little town that surrounded Birch College. My favorite coffee shop, Beans So Good, had become my home-away-from-dorm in freshman year. It was on the main street, only steps from the college. Liam pulled around to the back and parked near the dumpster.

"This incognito enough for you, princess?" He smirked at me.

"It's fine." I folded my arms over my chest as he opened his door.

"What do you want to drink?"

I considered refusing the offer, but the aroma from Beans drifted in on the cold air.

"Medium espresso, please. Two sugars. Splash of cream."

He climbed out. "Be right back."

Warmth began to seep into my bones from the leather seats. I lay my head back and closed my eyes as sleepiness washed over me. The toll of my stress over the last few days was catching up with me. Sitting here in Liam's car, drowsy and breathing his scent as it lingered, made me wonder why I'd gotten myself so worked up. What was the big deal, anyway? So he'd kissed me. So I'd kissed him back. It hadn't gone further than that, and no one had to know. We could laugh about it, share a cup of coffee and then forget it ever happened.

I jolted awake when the door open and Liam slid back inside. He handed me a foam cup as I struggled to sit up straight.

"Catching a nap?" He snapped back the tab on the lid of his cup and blew into the hole before sipping.

"Yeah. I haven't been sleeping well." I wanted to bite off my tongue. Why did I tell him that? So he could tease about giving me sleepless nights?

But to my amazement, Liam didn't make a smartass remark. He just shook his head.

"I don't know anyone who works as hard you do, Ava. I'm surprised you're not tired all the time."

I took an experimental drink of my coffee, noting that it was perfect. I was surprised that he'd managed to get it right; I hadn't given him specifics. Along with his remark about me working hard, he had caught me off-guard. I didn't realize Liam had noticed that much about me.

"I usually do okay." I hesitated a moment before going on. "But I've been a little distracted, I guess. I got a bad grade on a quiz today. I can't let that happen."

He put the car in gear, looking out the rear view mirror as he maneuvered out of the lot and back onto the street. "What did you get?"

I sighed. "I got a C on a quiz in cog psych."

Liam glanced at me with raised brows and wide eyes. "That's a bad grade?"

"It is for someone who has to maintain a certain average to keep her scholarship."

"I get that." He nodded, and I remembered that although Liam's family certainly had enough money to send a dozen kids through school, his roommate Giff was at Birch on the same type of scholarship I had.

"Anyway, I can't afford to take my focus off academics. So you've got to stop calling me and texting me. And waiting for me outside of classrooms." I held up my cup. "Even if you do bribe me with hot coffee."

He didn't answer, though his mouth thinned a little. I wondered where he was driving us, since we weren't going in the direction of campus. He turned down a side road and into a small park that sat on the edge of Gatbury. It was deserted today, and fields of untouched snow sprawled out white, dazzling even in the dull winter grayness.

Liam parked the car and picked up his coffee from the cup holder. We were both quiet for a few moments as he unfastened his seat belt and shifted to face me.

"I understand what you're saying." He finally spoke, staring out the windshield. "I'm sorry for being a distraction. I just ..." He rubbed a hand on his jean-covered knee. "I wanted to give this a chance. Like I said, I didn't mean to kiss you the other night, but once I did, I haven't been able to stop thinking about you."

"That's—" I shook my head. "Don't say stuff like that. I don't want to hear it. I feel guilty enough already."

"But I wanted you to know something. Last year, when I went out with Julia the first night, we had an okay time. She's cool, you know. Funny and pretty. And then I went to pick her up for our next date, and you were there. Do you remember that? She was running late. We talked about the Middle East after I told you I was a poli sci major."

"I remember." That night after Julia got back home, I had told her there was more to Liam Bailey than I'd expected.

"Julia and I talked about you at dinner. I wasn't sure I

41

wanted to let anything serious happen with her, and we got to talking about our roommates. She told me you were the smartest person she'd ever known, her best friend outside her sisters, and then she said you were the perfect roommate because you didn't date, so she never had to worry about strange guys being in her room. She said guys asked you out all the time, but you always said no. So I figured it was a lost cause. I'm not saying I kept going out with Julia for that reason only. Like I told you, we just kind of fell into it."

I closed my eyes. "I don't want to hear this, Liam."

"I didn't want to like you like that. But when everything else fell apart, all I could think was that now maybe I had a chance with you."

"Nothing has changed. I don't date. And if I did, I would never hurt Julia like that." I drained my cup.

"You told me she was okay. Why should she care?"

"It doesn't matter. It's the principle. Friends don't date friends' exes." I looked at the clock on the dash. "And I need to get back to the dorm. Jules is going to worry about me."

Liam put his coffee back in the holder and turned in his seat. "I want to go on record as saying that's a lame-ass reason not to go out with me. If you don't like me, don't want to be with me, that's one thing, but just because I went out with your friend? Stupid."

"I guess you're entitled to your opinion. Doesn't change anything."

"Yeah, it does, actually. It pisses me off. Because you know what, Ava? The other night, when I was kissing you, you were into it. You may be able to convince yourself that it was just me, that I surprised you, but that's bullshit."

The truth stung. "That doesn't prove a thing. I might not date, but it doesn't mean I'm made of stone. I'm human." *All too human*, I thought smothering a sigh.

"Really?" Liam leaned toward me, his eyes fastened on mine. "So did you enjoy kissing me?"

I flushed and dropped my eyes to stare at the console. "Please don't do this to me, Liam."

"Do what? Make you admit that you might have feelings for me, too?"

"Even if I did, I'm smart enough not to act on them." I had to remember who he was. No matter how steady his blue eyes were, how intoxicating he smelled ...this was still Liam.

"Why is that smart?"

"Because I know you're either lying to me or to yourself. Maybe to both of us. Because Saturday morning, not even twelve hours after you were lying on *my* bed kissing *me* senseless, you were offering Julia strings-free sex."

Liam froze. His eyes closed, and he swallowed hard.

"Did you think she wouldn't tell me that? What kind of a fool do you think I am?"

"No, I didn't think about it all." He raked his fingers through his hair. "I was mad at her. She's just so damned aggravating sometimes."

"That's a lot of passion for someone you claim not to care about. Maybe you need to rethink how you feel about Jules."

Liam shook his head. "She irritates me, like nails on a chalkboard. That's not passion." He reached across and snagged my hand, holding tight even when I tried to pull back. "You, on the other hand, make me crazy, until I just want to—do this."

He tugged me closer with the hand he still held, and before I could protest, he was kissing me. This wasn't the tentative and gentle kiss he'd started with the other night; this was full-on take over of my senses. His mouth was open over mine, his tongue making insistent forays against my lips until I parted them.

He slid his hand up my arm to the back of my neck and threaded his fingers through my hair, holding my head in place and angling his to cover my mouth more completely. My heart thudded until I was sure he could feel it, and the small voice that always kept me on the straight and narrow was drowned out by the blood rushing in my ears. A thrill of heat shot down my center, and I only wanted more. I wanted his hands down my body, the weight of him on top of me ...

My telephone buzzed in my pocket against my hip, jolting me to awareness. I leaned back away from Liam, flattening my hand on his chest when he made to follow me.

"Wait—my phone." I stretched to dig it out, arching my back to be able to reach it while Liam collapsed into his own seat with a groan.

"Julia's texting me. She wants to know where I am. God, what is wrong with me?" I dropped my head into hands, my phone on my lap.

"Nothing's wrong with you." Liam's hand ventured over to touch the back of my head, stroke down my mess of hair.

"Yes, there is. You're a terrible person because you brought me out here, and I'm a terrible person because I like kissing you. Take me back, please."

"Ava, you're not a terrible person. And neither am I. But you—hey, you admitted it."

"What?" I looked at him through my fingers.

He grinned at me, touching my cheek. "You said you like kissing me."

"Ugh!" I groaned and covered my face again. "You're incorrigible."

He laughed at me as he put the car in gear and pulled out of the park. "Maybe I am, but just remember, you're the one who likes kissing me.

JULIA COULD TELL something was wrong. I saw her watching me, an odd expression on her face, more than once over the rest of the week. I avoided her, going right to the library from class and adding a few extra study groups to my schedule. I decided it was penance for my sins. Plus maybe it would keep me from screwing up any more quizzes.

Liam kept up a steady stream of texts, pestering me until I answered. He showed up outside my class again, and after a little persuasion, I agreed to let him walk me to the library, as long as he kept his hands—and his lips—to himself.

But the guilt didn't go away.

Julia was gone all day Saturday at a journalism conference in Philadelphia. As much as I loved her, it was a relief to have the room to myself for a day. I hadn't told Liam that she was going to be away, because I was afraid he would show up and tempt me beyond my ability to say no.

I spent the morning dealing with a few freshman issues and putting together notes from our last RA meeting. Afterwards, I stripped the sheets from my bed and trundled them down to the laundry room. The sun shone through windows as I came back in, and I paused, watching the dust motes dance along a beam that ended on my desk. A framed photograph was nearly hidden by the pile of books. I reached for it, carefully smoothing my fingers over the glass. My sister's face smiled up at me, her dark eyes laughing, her mouth open as though she were about to share the joke.

A pain I'd thought had dulled to an ache squeezed my heart. I sat down at my desk, wishing I could have just five minutes more with Antonia. If I could call and ask her advice about this whole mess with Liam, I knew she'd help me see things clearly. Of course, if she were still around, maybe I wouldn't be the same Ava. Maybe I'd be the kind of girl who went on dates and kissed boys and didn't care about graduating with honors. I cold hardly remember that girl.

The rosary my grandmother had given me for confirmation usually hung over the frame. I retrieved it from where it had slipped down onto the desk and draped it on the corner. Fingering the small wooden beads, I had an idea.

I turned some music on over our sound system and dusted and vacuumed our room to the accompaniment of Frank Sinatra singing *The Girl from Ipanema.* Old school, yes, but I couldn't help the music I loved. I kept my Frank-obsession to a minimum when Julia was around, but alone I could listen all I wanted without her commentary.

Once the room was clean, I moved my sheets to the dryer, and then I got dressed and walked across campus to Our Lady of Mercy.

When I was growing up, my family had never missed a Sunday morning Mass. Father Byers was the priest who'd christened me and given me my First Holy Communion. He had been transferred before my confirmation, but to my surprise, it turned out he was rector at the church in Gatbury. My parents were overjoyed to know he was there; I think it gave them peace of mind, since they weren't able to see me often. I liked having someone familiar nearby, too.

Father Byers was in his office when I knocked on the door. He greeted me with a smile.

"Come in! Have a seat. What can I do for you?"

"I thought I'd come to mass today. And I wondered if you'd hear my confession beforehand, if you have time."

"Of course." He leaned back in his chair, studying me over the top of his glasses. "Is this a booth kind of confession, or a talk face-to-face confession?"

I sighed. "I think I'd rather stay in here, if you don't mind. I could use some guidance."

He nodded. "What's up?"

It only took a few minutes for me to pour out the abbreviated version of the last few weeks. Father Byers listened, but he didn't speak until I finished.

"So you're struggling because you feel guilty for having feelings toward your friend Julia's former boyfriend?"

"Yes. I mean, if they had just had a friendly break-up, I guess it wouldn't be so bad. But the way he treated her ...and how she feels toward him ...it's like I'm betraying her."

"Hmmm." He stared over my shoulder for a few minutes, rubbing his chin in silence. I sat still, knowing that he was deep in thoughtful prayer.

"Ava, I'm glad you're unhappy about this situation." I raised my eyebrows, but he waved his hand. "No, I know. But it's a sign that there's something going on that you need to address. I'm not sure I understand this girl code you talk about. I think you're afraid you might be betraying your friend, and that's a valid concern, since you haven't been honest with her."

"So do I tell her? What if she never speaks to me again? That would kill me."

"And what will happen when she finds out from someone else? Far better coming from you in the form of an apology."

I sighed long and hard. "You're right. Okay. I'll talk to her." I paused, toying with the edge of my scarf. "What about Liam? I need to walk away, right? Forget about him?"

Father Byers templed his fingers over his nose. "Is this Liam Catholic?"

I tried to remember if we'd ever discussed religion while he was going out with Julia. "I'm not sure. I don't think so."

The priest grimaced. "Well, if your mother asks, I advised you to find a good Catholic boy. Better yet, a good Catholic *Italian* boy. But for our purposes here, I think you should follow your heart. Within the teachings of the Church, of course."

I sighed. "It doesn't really matter, anyway. I don't have time for someone like Liam in my life. I can't risk losing my focus."

"Ava, I appreciate your dedication. I know your parents are proud of you. But try to remember that fun isn't necessarily sinful. It's all right to relax every once in a while."

When I didn't answer, Father Byers stood up. "Let me get my stole, and I'll give you absolution. Then I need to get ready to say Mass."

Ch♥pter Four

I KNEW FATHER Byers was right, and I needed to come clean to Julia. But still, I dragged my feet. After Mass, I hid out at the library for the rest of the afternoon. It was dark by the time I made a quick trip to Beans. I ordered my espresso and found a table in the back, where I opened my computer to work on my term paper.

"I thought I'd find you here."

I jerked my eyes from the screen to Liam's face. He stood across the table, his hands on the empty chair, grinning down at me.

"Liam, I'm busy. Please leave."

"I've been texting you all day, and you've been ignoring me. I thought we were past that."

"You might be, but I'm not. Nothing has changed. Except ..." I took a deep breath. "I'm going to talk to Jules and tell her everything. I can't keep lying to my best friend."

I'd half-expected Liam to protest, but as usual, he surprised me.

"Good. Then we don't have to sneak around."

I rolled my eyes. "You're missing the point. After I tell her, I'm not seeing you again."

"Why not? I thought your guilt trip was about not telling Julia."

"Do you ever listen to me?" I folded my napkin into a neat square. "I don't have time go out with you. I don't do romance, I don't go on dates, and that's final."

"Then what was the other day in the car? And that night in your room?"

"Temporary insanity. And now I'm cured." I finished my coffee and stood up. "Good-bye, Liam."

I chucked my cup in the trash, and I didn't look back as I walked out the door.

AS IT TURNED out, it was Tuesday before I talked to Julia. Between her dates with Jesse—things were definitely heating up there—and my class schedule, we kept missing each other. I didn't push the issue; the idea of having to confess all became scarier the more I thought about it.

She hijacked me Tuesday morning as I was getting ready for my early class, and we agreed to meet at Beans that afternoon. My stomach rolled ominously all day, and the closer the end of the day came, the worse I felt.

I arrived at the coffee shop first. It tended to get busy in the late afternoon, so I got in line, ordered our drinks and found a table before Julia even got there. I'd been sitting there, turning my Styrofoam cup in slow circles when I saw her come in. She scanned the room, and I waved to get her attention.

"Hey, there you are." She dropped her bag in the

empty chair and sat down across from me.

"I ordered you a mocha latte on ice. Even though I think you're crazy to drink cold stuff in the winter."

She laughed. "I'm quirky, what can I say? Thanks. And it's not that cold out today. The sun feels good."

"Yeah." I picked up the paper wrapper from my straw and began folding it into tiny geometric shapes. I swallowed hard over the lump in my throat.

"Ave." Jules caught my hand and squeezed it. "What's up? This is me. I know everything about you, and I love you anyway. Remember, I'm the one who's been driving you nuts being needy and insane the last three months."

I raised my eyebrow. "Only the last three months?"

She grinned. "Thanks, I love you, too. But seriously, tell me what's going on."

This was it. I took a deep breath and licked my dry lips. "Jules, I do love you. You know that, right? You're the best friend I've ever had. We might joke about that, but it's true. I would never, ever hurt you for anything in the world."

Julia frowned. "Okay, yeah, I know all that. Ave, you're freaking me out."

The smell of my espresso was making me nauseated. I pushed it away. "That Friday night, when you had your first date with Jesse, Liam came over as you were leaving."

She nodded. "Right. You said after I left, he just went on about me going out with other guys, blah, blah, blah. You told him to mind his own business."

"Yes. That's what happened." I took a deep breath. "To a certain point. When you left, he was standing in the hall. I didn't plan to let him into our room. He kept talking, and I was trying to get him to leave. And that girl Rachel—the freshman? She was walking by with a bunch of her friends. Liam didn't want her to see him, so he asked if he could come in for a minute. And he did."

I leaned my head into my hands. This next part would be easier if I didn't have to look Julia in the eye. "I swear, Jules, I never thought anything would happen. I figured he would finish what he was saying, I'd get him to leave, and I could go back to my homework. But then we got talking. I was giving him a hard time about Rachel, and he said nothing happened between them. It was a mistake."

Julia snorted. "Yeah, a big mistake he was making out with in front of all our friends just to shake me loose. What goes around ..."

I nodded, still not looking up. "I said pretty much the same thing. And he said it was more complicated than we knew, but he felt bad that you were making mistakes when it was his fault."

"Same old song. Ava, I still don't see—"

"I'm not finished." I spoke through clenched teeth. "After that, we were just talking. I had forgotten how much I used to enjoy that when you guys were dating. And then I got out some wine-coolers. And Liam started telling me about how he's not sure he wants to go into the career his parents want for him, and ...I don't even remember what I said, but the next thing I knew, he was kissing me."

For a moment, Julia was silent. I chanced a peek at her face. Her eyes were wide, and her mouth hung open.

"Oh my God! Are you freaking kidding me? And here I was thinking he might be changing. Ave, I am so sorry. He's an asshole."

It would have been easy to leave it that. But it wouldn't have been right.

I swallowed again. "Jules, you don't understand. It wasn't just him kissing me. I kissed him back. And

...more."

Jules leaned forward. "More? What do you ...Ava, did you sleep with him?"

"No." I shook my head. "But there was kissing. And touching."

Julia sat back in her chair, her hands flat on the table. I could see the shock and the anger, and I waited for her to blast me for my betrayal. Instead she looked into my eyes and sighed.

"Ava, I'm not mad. Not at you, anyway. I'm surprised. Shocked. I don't know what to say."

I leaned forward, needing her to understand. "I didn't, either. After he left, I felt stupid. I figured he was probably using me to get back at you for all the guys he thought you were seeing. But then he called and he texted, and he kept trying to talk with me."

She shook her head. "This is a mess. I get-I mean, I mostly get—how you could kiss him. He's hot, he's good and you're not the first girl he's conned into a make-out session or worse, I bet. I hope you told him to go to hell when he called you."

I twisted my fingers together. "I tried to. But he's been relentless. I actually saw him a few times this week." The memory of our kiss in the car at the park burned across my mind. "I feel stupid for doing it. I'm so, so sorry, Jules. Can you forgive me?"

She poked her drink with the straw. "There's nothing to forgive. I don't care about Liam. I only care about you. If I really thought you two could work, I'd deal with it. But we know Liam. He'll only break your heart."

I sniffed as tears threatened. "Everyone knows you don't make out with your best friend's ex. Ever. What's the matter with me? I'm a horrible bitch."

"You are not. Liam is a master manipulator. I just

wish you'd told me right away, so you didn't have to agonize over it." She paused, drawing circles on the side of her damp cup. "Ava ...why didn't you tell me? You're not interested in going out with him, are you?"

I thought of Liam's hand holding mine, the laughter in his eyes as we talked. And I pushed it away. "Of course not. It was temporary insanity, I guess." I repeated the same words I'd given him.

Jules nodded. "Okay." She stared down at the table, and I knotted my hands. I had thought that coming clean to Julia was going to make everything better, and I did feel a sense of relief. But a strange heaviness had also settled down in the pit of my stomach, as though I had lost something I'd never had.

THERE WAS AN odd, almost uncomfortable quiet between Julia and me as we walked to our room. She disappeared to take a shower once we were back inside, and I changed into yoga pants and a hoodie. I climbed into bed, slipped in my earbuds and turned on music. I hit my favorite go-to play list, heavy on the Frank Sinatra tunes, and his *Body and Soul* poured into my ears. Anything to drown out the pain.

A chirp interrupted my song, and I glanced down at the message from Liam.

Did you tell her?

I began to delete it, and then changed my mind. He deserved to know that much, I decided.

Yes. It's fine.

Go out with me tonight. I'll meet you somewhere.

I closed my eyes and took a deep breath. I pushed away the memories of Liam's laugh, his eyes when he looked at me, the feel of his lips over mine ...and instead, I chose to think about only all the terrible things he had done. Intentionally hurting Julia. Making poor Rachel the freshman cry. All the girls he'd dated and tossed away before he and Jules got together. I had to be strong, and in order to do that, I had to focus on the bad.

No.

I hit send, and then I went back and deleted all of his texts from my phone. I opened my Behavior Disorders book and started reading as Julia came in, bringing steamy air from her shower. I was vaguely aware of her as she dried her hair and pulled out her own homework. But I was preoccupied until a pillow hit me in the head.

I jumped and pulled out my earbuds. "What was that for?"

"It's dinner time. Want me to get takeout? You look pretty snuggled down there."

I shrugged. "Whatever. I'm not hungry."

She climbed into bed with me. "What's wrong? You're not still worried I'm mad, are you? I'm not."

I pressed my lips together and shook my head. "I'm disappointed in myself. All this time, I've been focusing on school stuff, getting good grades, keeping my scholarship. I guess part of me thought I was above all that boy stuff. I stick to my path, and I don't give dating a thought. Well, not much, anyway. But then some guy who I know is a jerk and a player comes along and kisses me, and I'm no better than any other lovesick girl."

"Lovesick?" Julia raised her eyebrows at me.

I flushed. "A figure of speech."

She laid her head on my shoulder. "Ave, you're the most amazing person I know. You're gorgeous, smart and funny. All you'd have to do is let it happen, and guys would be falling at your feet. But you have a plan, and you stay focused. Just because you have one little slip-up doesn't mean you've failed. I can tell you Liam Bailey isn't just a typical guy. He might be a class-A ass, but the boy knows how to kiss. And what to say to a girl, when he's in the mood to be charming. So don't beat yourself up."

I closed my eyes and dropped my head back. This was not helping me forget the parts of Liam that tempted me.

Julia sat up. "I didn't tell you. I had a meeting today with Dr. Turner. I've decided not to write that story for the blog. At least, I'm not naming names."

"What made you change your mind?" I turned on my side and pulled the blanket up over my arm.

She shook her head. "I don't know. I guess it was realizing that I've moved on. I had such a good time with Jesse last night. It's easy, and it feels right, you know? Not the constant up and down and angst there was with Liam. I ran it all by Dr. Turner, and she gave me some good advice."

"So all the revenge plans are abandoned?" I caught the side of my lip between my teeth.

"I guess. When I saw him this afternoon, I--"

I sat up fast, almost knocking Julia off the bed in the process.

"You saw Liam this afternoon?"

"Yeah. Sorry, I guess I forgot, with us talking about everything else. He was standing outside the building here when I got back from seeing Dr. Turner."

"What was he doing here?"

Jules shook her head. "I have no idea. He was kind of cagey about it. No, that's not true. He was, like, nervous. And he apologized for the other day. I mean, really said he was sorry, not the typical cover-his-ass-and-not-take-any-blame crap. I almost fell over."

"He apologized?"

"Yeah, for what that's worth."

My mind began to race. I needed to get Liam out of my system, off my mind, once and for all. He wasn't going to give up as long as he thought there was a chance for us—and clearly I wasn't very good at being firm when I was with him. But maybe there was a way to convince him, give Jules her payback and get my life on track again.

"Jules, what would you think about throwing another birthday party?"

She stared at me. "What do you mean?"

"My birthday is in two weeks. Give me a party. And we'll both get what we want. You'll have revenge, and I'll get him to leave me alone."

"Ava, that's crazy."

"No, it's not. It's perfect. Everything else we were thinking about before was so haphazard—you showing up all over campus with different guys hoping to make him jealous, even writing about him on the blog—all of that felt sloppy. But this, this is exactly right."

She wrinkled her forehead, and her lips tightened. "It's not fair to you. Ave, you don't need to do this."

"Oh, I think I do. And it's fair to me. He decided to include me in his games. He wants to mess with me? Good. Now it's time for him to get a big old tablespoon of his own medicine."

"The last thing I want to do is plan another birthday party." Jules groaned. "You know what people are going to be saying. It'll bring up everything from December

57

again."

"Exactly. So it'll be fresh in people's minds. And when Liam walks in, every eye will be on him."

"Ava, are you sure ...?"

I squeezed her arm. "Stop it, Jules. I'm positive. Get the girls on the floor to help you with the decorations. You can handle the food. We can have it in the main lounge here. And don't worry about Liam. I'll deliver a special invitation to him."

Julia shook her head. "God, Ave, you scare me. Remember you're supposed to use your powers for good, not evil."

I laughed. "This is for the good. Liam Bailey is going to learn what happens when you screw with the wrong women."

Ch♥pter Five

THE MAIN LOUNGE in our dorm was wall-to-wall crepe paper and balloons. Letting fifty freshman girls loose with decorations and a helium tank might not have been a good idea, but at least the room looked ...festive.

Julia stood in the middle of the chaos, pointing at people, yelling directions and ogling her boyfriend as he carried in an ice chest. It made me smile; the last few weeks had been rough on the two of them. As I had predicted, the original revenge plan had turned around to bite Jules in the ass when Jesse heard rumors that his new girlfriend was dating every guy on campus. It had taken a lot of explanation on her part and understanding on his before they settled everything.

In the process, Julia had promised that she wouldn't try for payback against Liam anymore. So as far as she and Jesse knew, tonight was just my birthday party, pure and simple. I didn't want to make it any different, although neither of them knew I hadn't abandoned my own, more subtle plans for finally getting Liam out of my system.

He hadn't given up on me, even when I refused to

answer his calls. So it wasn't hard to send him a quick text at the last minute, inviting him to the party Julia was throwing. He'd answered right away.

I'll be there.

"Ava, you looked beautiful." Julia hugged me and then held me out at arms' length. She inspected me head to toe. We'd spent hours taming my black hair into manageable fat curls without a hint of frizz. It fell perfectly over my shoulders, which were bared in the flirty little black dress I'd found at the thrift shop.

"Everything in here looks so pretty. Thank you so much for all of this." I smiled up into the dimpled face of her boyfriend. "I'm glad you're here, Jesse. It's going to be fun tonight."

Jules leaned back against Jesse's chest. "I hope so. As long as you're happy, so am I. You deserve a kick-ass party."

"That's just what this is going to be." Jesse threaded his fingers through Julia's and leaned to kiss her neck. I looked away to hide my sudden stab of envy. I was happy for my friend; Jesse was a keeper. And I wasn't looking for a relationship, I reminded myself. I just wanted my boring old life back. Tonight was the first step in making that happen.

"Jules! Everything looks perfect." Giff came up behind me and reached around to hug Jules. "You're getting to be a pro. Parties by Julia. Nah, that's too plain. I'll have to come up with something better."

"Yeah, no thanks. I think I'll keep my day job." Julia smiled. "At least no one's going to be surprised at this one. I hope."

Giff laughed, and Julia introduced him to Jesse. When a freshman came up in a panic about missing napkins, Jules excused herself to help. Giff turned to me.

"There's the birthday girl. Looking gorgeous as always, peaches." He leaned down to kiss my cheek. "Ava, when are you going to give in and let me set you up with the perfect guy? All you have to do is say yes, and I can make it happen."

I laughed. "Thanks, but no. You know my rules. Graduate with honors, get the degree, get the job ...and then maybe I'll have time for men."

He shook his head. "All work and no play ...is a waste of all this beauty."

"Ah, Giff." I patted his arm. "You're good for my ego. Now fill me in on this new guy in your life. Jules says he's pretty awesome."

Giff and I chatted until a few people I knew from class came over to say hello. I began to relax and enjoy myself. Julia waved to me with a smile as she headed over to check on the food, which was just being laid out on the long tables.

And then an abrupt silence crashed over the room. I caught the expression on Giff's face as he looked toward the door, and I knew.

Julia's face froze. She knew that I had invited Liam, but she hadn't expected him to show up. Or maybe the overwhelming sense of déjà vu was hitting her. Everyone in the room was watching, waiting to see what they would do.

Liam glanced over the crowd, but he didn't move until he spotted me. His eyes fastened on my face, and skimmed down my body. I felt a flush of heat, as though he were touching me. He took half a step toward me and then stopped.

Julia came from behind me and threaded her way through groups of people. She held her head high, smiling. She paused in front of him, and then held out her hand.

"I'm so glad you could make it, Liam. Come on, get something to eat." She looked back at me. "Ava's over there. I'm sure you want to tell her happy birthday." She raised her voice to encompass the room, "Let's eat up, everyone! I'm bringing out the cake in about half an hour."

The spell of silence broke as guests surged toward the tables. Julia touched my shoulder as she passed by me on her way back to Jesse's side, but I didn't move.

"Hey, birthday girl, let's get you a plate." Giff came up next to me. "Quick, before the freshman vermin devour it all."

I forced a smile. "Okay. Good idea."

He glanced down at me, curiosity in his eyes. "You okay?"

"Yeah. Just ..." I whooshed out a breath. "You know. Weird. After last time." I looked over at Liam, who had turned to join the food line.

"Oh, right. Well, I like to think that maybe our boy is leaning how to behave and play nice. I didn't know he was coming tonight, by the way. I hope Jules knows I didn't tell him about it."

"It's all good. Let's eat."

Everything was delicious, and Giff was right—it was gone in short order. They brought in the cake, and everyone sang to me while I kept a smile pasted on my face. I cut slices until everyone had some and then took my own plate into the corner to sit with Giff.

I was just licking the last bits of frosting off my plastic fork when I felt Liam's hand on my shoulder.

"Happy birthday, Ava."

I looked up, intent on keeping my face expressionless. "Thank you, Liam."

Across the room, someone called for Giff. He hesitated, glancing at me.

"Go ahead, I'm fine." I watched as he joined a crowd of guys Julia and I had met earlier this year.

Liam dropped into the chair he'd vacated. "So. Nice party."

"Yes. Julia has a knack for them."

"Ava ...I'm glad you invited me tonight." He reached across the table and touched my arm. "Go out with me tonight, after everyone leaves. We'll go get a drink. Or coffee."

I sighed. "Don't ruin this, please."

"I don't want to ruin anything. I want to spend time with you."

"Why? I've made it clear how I feel. Stop wasting your time, Liam." I tossed the words out as a test, wondering how he would respond. I was playing a risky game, and the deeper I got, the more I began to dread how it would end. I kept telling myself that I wanted him to leave me alone, but right now, sitting so close to him ...I wasn't so sure.

He didn't answer, but he didn't move away, either. People were beginning to leave, and a few stopped to hug me and wish me happy birthday again. Most looked at Liam with open curiosity, but he ignored them all.

I followed the direction of his gaze across the room, to where Jesse had Julia wrapped in his arms as she looked up at him. He caught me watching him.

"What are you doing after this is over?" His voice was low and tugged at a yearning low in my center.

"Nothing. Going back to my room, getting ready for bed, I guess."

"Is Julia going to be there?"

I was torn between telling the truth and protecting

myself. What I wanted was becoming less clear by the minute.

"No," I said finally. "She's going home with Jesse." This was going to be their first overnight together, and Jules was both nervous and excited.

"Can I come over, then? I promise, I'll behave. I won't push. I'll sit across the room from you if that's what you want."

I played with the edge of the plastic tablecloth as two voices within me warred for supremacy. Liam leaned forward and laid his arm over the table, with his hand palm up near mine.

"Please?" The whisper caressed my ear and slid down my spine. Before I could think about it anymore, I nodded.

T HE GOOD THING about living in a freshman dorm was that we had ready labor. Just as the girls had helped organize and set up my birthday party, they also stayed to pitch in on cleaning up.

"Are you sure you don't want me to stay and supervise?" Julia stood in the hall with Jesse, looking over my shoulder into the lounge. "It's your birthday, you shouldn't have to work."

I gave her a little shove. "Go. My minions are on it. I won't have to lift a finger. And with any luck, this will tire them all out, and they won't have the energy to get into trouble and bother me the rest of the weekend. You two ..." I pointed at them. "Shoo, shoo. Take her home with you, Jesse. Force her to relax."

The slow smile the spread across his face made me blush, and I shook my head and hid my eyes. "I don't want details. Just go."

Jules laughed. "Okay, we're going. I'll see you around dinner tomorrow, right? Jesse's sister is coming down for lunch. I get to meet her." The tone of her voice didn't match her words. I knew Jesse's mother and sister, who lived in New York, were less than enthusiastic about him dating someone down in South Jersey, and Julia was nervous about the whole thing.

"She's going to love you. Why wouldn't she? Have fun. And thank you again, both of you." I hugged my roommate and then stood on tiptoe to kiss Jesse's cheek. "Take care of my girl here."

It didn't take long for the freshman to fill several trash bags and carry them down to the dumpster. I did a once-over inspection to make sure everything was back in order before I let them go.

Liam had disappeared at some point during the clean-up process. I wondered if he had changed his mind about coming over tonight, and I tried not to care.

The halls were relatively quiet as I made my way back to my room. A group of girls swung around the corner, still dressed up, heading out. They waved to me.

"Great party, Ava! Happy birthday again."

I smiled. Sometimes looking at freshman made me feel ancient. They were so enthusiastic and ...young. I caught sight of a familiar face in the crowd of girls. Rachel the freshman was giggling with one of her friends. She glanced over at me and grinned as they chattered. Apparently, her broken heart was healing.

I unlocked my door and flipped on the light, kicking off the heels that had been torturing my poor feet all night. The room was quiet without Julia, and I mused that I had better get used to it. I had a feeling that she was going to be spending most of her time with Mr. Tall, Sweet and

Dimpled from now on.

I put away my shoes and had just shut the closet door when I heard a soft knock. My pulse skittered, even as I sternly warned myself that it was probably just a stray freshman girl who needed my wisdom.

I took a deep breath, opened the door and tried not to grin like a fool when I saw Liam standing on the other side, leaning against the jam with his hands behind his back.

"Hey." His eyes trailed down from my face, running along my body. When he made his way back to my eyes, he smiled. "Can I come in?"

"Oh. Yeah." I stood back out of the way, and he stepped inside, closing the door. Julia and I had the biggest room on the floor, but strangely, with Liam standing in it with me, it felt much too small.

"Happy birthday." He brought his hands around, and in one of them was a perfect pink rose.

"Ohhhh." I took it, careful of the thorns, and brought to my nose, sniffing deep. "It's beautiful. But you didn't have to."

He lifted one shoulder. "I wanted to. I'd like to take you out to dinner to celebrate your birthday, but I have a feeling you'd say no. So ...this is what I did."

I stood rooted to the floor, staring down at the flower. I'd never gotten a flower from a boy before. Almost involuntarily, I stroked it along my cheek, feeling the velvet softness against my skin.

Liam made a noise in his throat, almost a strangled sound. I glanced up into eyes that were full of fire and an intense want.

"I should put this in water," I whispered and turned to the small cabinet. All we had were our fancy red plastic cups, so I pulled out one of those and filled it with water from the bathroom. Liam didn't move, but I felt his eyes on me as I set the cup on my desk. When I turned back, he reached one finger to trace down my arm.

"You look so beautiful tonight." He caught my fingers between his own. "I don't think I've ever seen you dressed up like this."

"Thanks." My tongue darted out to touch my lip. "You look good, too."

And he did. He wore a long-sleeved button-up dress shirt with his jeans. The collar was open, and the cuffs were turned up so that I could see his forearms.

Liam tugged gently on the hand he held, pulling me closer so that my hip bumped against his leg.

"I thought you were going to stay far away, across the room from me." I felt I had to say it, even if I knew there was no way it was going to happen.

Liam smirked. "I said I would if you wanted me to. Do you want me to?" Before I could answer, or even think about answering, he dipped his head to kiss along the side of my neck.

I couldn't help myself. My arms went up around his back, and my head tilted to the side, giving him better access. He moved his hands to my back, fitting me closer to him as my breasts pressed against the hard muscled wall of his chest.

"What do you think, Ava ...should I go stand on the far side of the room?" He made his way to my mouth, and when I opened my lips to answer, he took advantage of the chance to kiss me, moving with knee-buckling slowness.

I was standing on my toes now to get as close as I could. Liam's right hand spread over my lower back, pressing me into him. His left hand tangled in the back of my hair, fingers caressing my scalp.

It had been so long since I'd given myself to being

touched like this, other than my all-too-brief kisses with Liam over the last weeks. But tonight, the guilt and confusion that had clouded those times were gone. I wanted his hands on me. I wanted to kiss him until I couldn't breathe, until I forgot my own name.

He groaned as he slid his hand from my neck, down my back and around to my side. My heart stuttered as his fingers teased at the bottom of my breast, covered only with the thin black material of the dress. I twisted, wanting more.

"Can we sit down?" He murmured the words against my ear, sending goose-bumps down my spine. I nodded, and he scooped me into his arms, carrying me to my bed. He sat down, laying me across his lap, as his lips trailed over my face.

I let myself touch his jaw, and then flattened one hand against his broad chest. I could feel the movement of muscle through the cotton of his shirt. But it wasn't enough. I wanted the warmth of his skin against my palm, so I slid my fingers to the buttons, fumbling to undo them.

"God, Ava, you are so beautiful. So fucking beautiful." Liam used one teasing finger under the thin string strap of my dress. "Your skin is like ...milk."

"Really? Milk?" I made a face. "I'm not much of a milk-drinker."

He kissed my neck, his lips curving into a smile. "Okay. Not milk. Umm ...alabaster?"

"Do you even know what that is?"

"As a matter of fact, I do. But maybe ..." He eased the strap down, lowering just the one side until the top of my breast was bared. "One year my parents took me to Anguilla, in the Carribbean. The sand on the beaches there is amazing. So soft and white, like powder, and warm ...that's what your skin reminds me of most. I wanted to sink into that sand for the rest of my life." His eyes captured mine, and I couldn't speak.

Then, bending his neck over me, with my head still resting in the crook of his other arm, he kissed down the exposed skin of my breast until his tongue met the edge of the fabric that hid my nipple. I lay perfectly still, almost afraid to breathe.

He straightened until he was looking down into my eyes again, replacing his lips with a single finger that drew a sensual circle over the silk, around the already-stiff peak. I arched my back, and the dress fell away. Liam muttered something I didn't understand and dropped his open mouth to the small pink bud.

The feeling of his tongue stroking the tip of my nipple as his mouth sucked hard drove me crazy. I wriggled in his lap, restless and wanting so much more. My hip jutted against the zipper of his jeans, straining with the proof of his desire.

I hadn't thought ahead, hadn't planned how far I was willing to go tonight. Being impulsive was a foreign concept to me, and it made me nervous. Part of me didn't want to think; it just wanted to feel and experience and touch. But the other side of me, the part that was growing increasingly alarmed, was yelling for me to wait. To consider this, what not stopping might mean. What it had meant before.

But to my surprise, I didn't have to be the one to slow us down. Liam moved his mouth, kissing up to my collarbone, and pulled my dress back over to cover me. He pushed back until he was sitting against the wall and propped me up so that my face was close to his. And then he dropped his head back on long, deep sigh.

"I don't want to stop." He spoke with his eyes closed as his fingers rubbed my hip. "If I could, I'd lay you down here on this bed and kiss every inch of your body ...I'd make you come until you forgot your own name. I'd lose myself in you for hours."

My mouth went dry, and I may have actually whimpered.

"But that's not what you really want."

I wasn't so sure about that.

"You'd be upset after. And I don't want you to think that's all I'm interested in. I want to take you out. I want to have dinner with you, and talk about politics, history, psychology ...all the shit that makes your eyes get bright when I bring it up."

I nodded, even though I wasn't sure I didn't want him to go back to the first part. The part about kissing every inch of my body.

Liam brushed my hair back from my face and looked down into my eyes. "I'm not sure what's going on in your head. Hell, I don't even know what I'm thinking. But I want to figure it out."

He kissed me again, holding my head in his hands, letting his lips rub languorously against mine. I relaxed into his arms, letting him move me at will.

At some point, I snuggled down into Liam's chest and dozed off. Only when my back protested my position did I wake up.

Liam's eyes were closed, and his head had lolled to the side. When I shifted and stretched my legs, he smiled. My heart lurched at that moment, and an odd feeling crashed over me. I didn't want to think about what it was.

"Sorry. Guess I fell asleep."

I rolled over and stood up, straightening my wrinkled dress. Liam climbed off the bed as well, checked the clock on Julia's desk.

"Holy shit, it's three in the morning." He grinned and

lifted a strand of my hair. "You really wore me out."

My face reddened, and he laughed. "I guess I better go."

I wondered if he wanted me to invite him to stay with me. It was almost morning anyway, and a few more hours wouldn't make much of a difference. While the college administration officially frowned on resident advisors having overnight visitors of the opposite sex, I knew they also looked the other way. No one was going to turn me for having Liam Bailey in my room.

But I didn't say anything. I was still too unsure about this whole situation. What I had planned to do to Liam was hazy now. After what he'd said to me tonight ...I needed time and space to think. To clear my brain.

"Will Giff be worried about you?" I ventured to ask.

Liam shook his head. "Nah, he probably crashed over at Jeff's. And it's not like we check in with each other."

I stood awkwardly in the center of the room. "You didn't wear a coat, did you?"

"I left it in the car. It's all right, I'm parked pretty close."

"Okay."

"Ava?"

I met his eyes.

"It's fine. I don't expect you to invite me to stay over."

I shrugged. "I would, it's just ..." My voice trailed off. "I don't know."

He smiled again. "How about a good-night kiss, then I'll let you get some sleep?"

I stepped closer and let him pull me to my tip-toes. His lips were warm and his tongue tempting, but he kept the kiss brief and released my arms.

"I'll call you tomorrow. Sleep well."

I managed a smile. "Thank you for my rose. And for

...everything."

Liam winked and opened the door. I fought down the temptation to follow and watch him down the hallway. Instead, I locked my door and leaned against it with sigh.

Shit. What now? What the hell did I do now?

Ch♥pter Six

T HE SUN WOKE me up the next morning, shining in my eyes at an angle that told me I'd slept late. Groaning, I buried my face in the pillow. I felt hung-over, even though I hadn't had anything at all to drink the night before. All I'd had was Liam, and way too much of him. Or maybe not enough.

Coffee. I needed a coffee, and as soon as possible. I slithered out of bed, pulled on my oldest, most comfortable jeans and the oversized hoodie that sagged almost to my knees. My hair was unholy mess, so I pulled it back into a messy bun and hoped like hell I didn't run into anyone I knew.

I could've hit the dining hall, but it was just as far away as Beans was. I knew Beans had better coffee, plus was a better place to hide out. I grabbed my jacket and my sunglasses and tucked my phone into my back pocket.

The line of people at the coffee shop was mostly made up of locals. I ordered my espresso and chocolate croissant and skulked back to my favorite corner table with the Sunday newspaper.

"Ava? Is that you?"

Shit. It was a girl I knew from the resident advisors board. I pasted on a smile. "Hi, Cary. How are you?"

"Oh, fine, thanks. Great party last night."

I had forgotten she was there. "Thanks. My room-mate Julia did a great job, and the freshman pitched in without too much complaining."

"Good to know. There's got to be some benefit to dealing with all the spats and broken hearts."

"Not to mention the first-time drunks and hang-overs."

"True." She leaned against the empty chair across from me. "So I was surprised to see Liam Bailey there last night. Didn't he date your roommate for a long time?"

I bit back a groan. "Yeah, they went out. But you know, we're all friends, so ..."

"Really? I heard they had a nasty breakup, that he cheated with some freshman chick."

I held Cary's gaze, refusing to give in. None of her damn business. "You know how these things get blown out of proportion."

"Yeah. Mostly. But with Liam, I'd believe anything." She made a face and hooked a thumb at her own chest. "Sophomore year. We met at a party at Alpha Delt. Had me convinced he was in love with me, that I was going to change his life. Ha!"

I felt the blood drain down to my feet. "He used to get around quite a bit, I know."

"It was more than that. He really chased me for three weeks. Called all the time, came to see me ...I was dumb enough to think I was going to be the one to hook him." She shook her head. "Hook up, yes. Hook him? Not so much. One night and he never spoke to me again."

I felt sick. "That's not cool. I'm sorry."

She shrugged. "It happens. Gave me a good story to warn my freshman girls away from dicks, right? Anyway ...I'll catch you at the next RA meeting."

I wanted to curl up on the floor and die. Idiot. I was such a fucking idiot. Thank God I hadn't actually slept with him. But this was almost worse.

I might not have fucked him, but I'd fallen for him.

BACK IN MY room, I paced the floor. I didn't know what to think. Cary didn't have any reason to tell me that story about Liam and her; she was dating someone now, a grad student, I was pretty sure. But everything happened for a reason. Maybe it wasn't coincidence that I'd run into her this morning, when I was still floating from my night with Liam.

This was what happened when I deviated from the path I'd chosen. Long ago I'd decided to stay away from guys until I was ready to be in control. Keeping my eyes on the prize, sticking to my guns—all of that had made me safe.

I picked up Antonia's picture and studied it. I remembered my bright-eyed sister, dancing, singing, cooking with our mother and me, laughing at life. Nothing had been the same since ...well, since.

That was why I had to stick to the plan. Schoolwork. Good grades. Graduating with honors. Using my psych degree to land a big-time job with a good salary at a top advertising agency. And then ...maybe a guy. But not until then.

The rose Liam had brought me sat on my desk behind my sister's photograph. I couldn't bring myself to throw it away, but I shoved it back behind some books so I didn't have to see it. And then I retrieved my notebooks and went back to my homework, the one place I felt safe and secure.

My phone stayed silent all day, which only confirmed to me what I'd feared. Liam didn't ever plan to call me. I was just part of his games. He must have gotten a good laugh at stupid Ava, who let him kiss and grope her after all her protests to the contrary.

Julia got home around six, a little subdued after her lunch with Jesse's sister.

"Allison was really nice," she assured me. "I mean, she seemed to be. She loves Jesse, for sure. And the few times she relaxed enough to be herself, I liked her. But she's so defensive about her mom, and she won't hear anything nice about Sarah and Danny. Or even poor Desmond."

I tried to listen and make the appropriate sympathetic noises. Julia had been working for Jesse's dad and stepmom as a nanny to their little boy Desmond for a long time now, and she was practically part of the family, even before she met Jesse. I knew there were some bad feelings between Jesse's parents, and his sister had taken their mother's side. Jesse was in the middle, more so since he'd come down to get his graduate degree at Birch and live with his father and Sarah. Even though it made perfect sense—he was getting a free ride plus room and board by getting his masters here—his mother saw it as a betrayal.

"How about you? What did you do today?" Jules finally stopped talking about lunch long enough to look at me.

"Homework. I had a quiet day. I needed it after all the fun last night." I gave her a sunny smile.

"Okay, good. I'm glad it went well, Ava. And I'm happy we're back, you know?" She hugged me, leaning awkwardly over my books and computer. "I don't want us to ever let a boy come between us. Especially not someone like Liam Bailey. Totally not worth it."

I nodded and changed the subject.

It was nearly midnight before my phone buzzed a text. My lips tightened as I read the message.

Hey, gorgeous. Sorry I didn't call today.

I drew in a deep breath. I knew what I had to do, but I needed some time to gear up for it. I had to play along for a little while.

No problem, I was pretty busy.

Lunch tomorrow?

I paused, my fingers hovering over my phone's keyboard.

I've got a full week. Lots of tests and a huge paper due. Can we say Friday night?

His reply was fast.

Sure. I'll miss you 'til then.

I raised my lips in a sneer. "Sure you will," I muttered.

"Ave?" In the dark, Julia's sleepy voice floated over to me. "Did you say something?"

"Just talking to myself, sorry. 'Night."

L IAM TEXTED ME sporadically throughout the week. I kept my replies short and non-committal, but pleasant. I didn't want him to come over before I was ready for him, and I didn't want him to suspect that I was at all upset.

On Wednesday night, Julia came into our room after work and dropped her bag on the bed with a deep sigh.

"She wants to meet me. Jesse's mom, I mean."

I glanced over at her from my closet, where I'd been hanging clean clothes. "That's a good thing, isn't it?"

"I don't know. I guess Allison was talking about us having lunch last weekend, and now Jesse's mother is flipping out because she's the last person in the family to meet me."

"Is she coming down here?" I found that unlikely, since I knew she didn't like Jesse's dad and his wife Sarah.

Julia shook her head. "No, we're driving up there. Jesse asked me this afternoon if I'd go up there with him." She pressed her hand to her stomach. "God, Ava, I'm going to be a nervous wreck."

"But you'll go anyway?" I smiled.

"Of course. For Jesse, I'd be willing to meet a hundred scary moms."

"That's sweet." I turned back to the closet, but the wheels in my mind were whirling. This was going to work out perfectly for me.

And it did. Julia left with Jesse right after work on Friday night. Liam had texted me that he'd be over at seven.

He knocked on the door at seven on the dot. My stomach turned over, and I looked toward Antonia's picture for strength. It was time to do this. Get it over with, end it, and move on with my life, the way I wanted to live it. I straightened my shoulders.

Liam leaned down to kiss me when I opened the door, but I turned my face so that his lips caught my cheek.

"Hey, beautiful. I missed you."

"Did you?" I gave him a small, tight smile and walked away to sit in the safety of my desk chair.

"Yeah." He frowned at me and jammed his hands into the pockets of his brown jacket. "How was your week?"

I lifted one shoulder. "Oh, you know. Typical. Busy."

"What's going on, Ava? You look ...strange."

"Strange?" I raised one eyebrow. "Oh, I'm sorry. Did you expect me to be waiting for you in bed? Was this the night you talked me into sleeping with you, and then you ditch me? Sorry. Didn't mean to ruin your plans."

"What the hell are you talking about?"

"Stop it, Liam. Please. Just stop. I want you to leave, and I want you to leave me alone."

"What happened? I thought ...when I left here last week, I thought we were good."

"I had a momentary lapse. Now I'm better."

"Is this how it's going to work for us? We make out, you let me kiss you, then you push me away and plead temporary insanity?"

"Nope. Not any more. I'm done. I want you to leave, and I don't want you to bother me again."

Liam shoved one hand through his hair. "Ava, come on. I just want to talk."

I closed my eyes. "Liam, no. Please. Go away."

"You can't tell me you don't feel anything for me. God, Ava, when I kiss you ...it's like everything in the world disappears. I don't want to stop. Ever."

"Well, you have to!" I tried to keep my voice down so as not to alarm the curious freshman girls.

"Why?" He moved closer, reaching to touch me, but I ducked away. I couldn't let him touch me. It robbed me of the ability to think clearly.

"Because, Liam, this is wrong. You don't care for me. You've talked yourself into thinking you do, for some reason I just don't understand. But you don't know me, and I'm not picking up for you where Julia left off. You forget, I saw firsthand how miserable you made her. No, thanks. I'm not signing up for that tour."

He sighed. "It's not the same. Julia and I were a mistake. I told you that. But Ava, I have never felt about anyone the way I feel about you. Just give me a chance to prove it."

I felt like screaming, and I tried to hold onto to Cary's words as they echoed in my head. *He had me convinced he was in love with me, that I was going to change his life.* But the voice that was telling me to take a chance, to let him in, was getting stronger. Pretty soon it would drown out the other voice, the sensible one that remembered that Liam Bailey was a jerk, and I would give in again, let him kiss me, touch me ...

"No." I said it out loud to strengthen my resolve. "Not again. Not this time." I tightened my jaw and swallowed. It was time to play my last card, the one that would get rid of Liam once and for all.

"Liam, you think you really like me, don't you?" I forced lightness into my voice. "You think it's different with us, right?"

"Yes." He spoke with relief, and I knew he thought that I was hearing him at last.

"Good." I clenched my fists against the seat of the wooden chair. "I'm glad. Because now I can tell you ..." I took a deep breath and plunged in. "I don't feel anything for you. Nothing but ...pity." I let that sink in. "After what you did to my best friend, did you seriously think I could even look at you? I've been playing you, Liam. Just waiting for this moment. You know what they say about revenge, right? Well, it's been worth the wait."

I finally raised my eyes to his face. Pain and another

emotion I didn't recognize warred behind his eyes, and I had to steel myself not to cross the room to hold him, to reach up and kiss away the hurt.

"That's it?" His words were clipped. "This was all a way to get back at me? You expect me to believe that?"

"Believe it or not. It's the truth." I bit the inside of my mouth hard, holding back the sobs that were gathering in my chest. I had to be strong for just a few more minutes, just until he left the room.

"I thought ...I thought this was different. *We* were different. But the whole time, this was just a game to you."

I couldn't speak any more. I nodded.

Liam turned. He paused for a minute in the doorway of the room, and for a crazy beat of my heart, I prayed he would come back in, see me for the liar I was.

But he didn't. He kept walking, away from me, out of my life.

When I knew I could move again without running after him, I walked across the room, closed the door behind him and locked it. Then I climbed into my bed, curled up on my side, and cried into my pillow, deep, silent sobs wracking my body until the whole bed shook.

Revenge was not sweet. It felt like death, and it hurt worse than anything I had ever known.

PART II

Ch♥pter Seven

Two months later

"AVA! WHERE HAVE you been, lovely? I haven't seen you in too long."

I turned, the smile on my face genuine for once.

"Hey, Giff. I've been around. Just busy with papers and school, you know. And it seemed like every single girl in our dorm had her second-semester-freshman-year meltdown the same week. It's been crazy."

He rolled his eyes. "Yeah, I hear you. Guys don't do the meltdowns. They just up the partying. I had three cases of alcohol poisoning in two weeks. So then I had to do the dorm meetings and the PSAs on the dangers of over-indulging. Fun times."

Someone bumped into me, and Giff caught my arm to keep me from going over. The student union was crowded, and we were standing in the main flow of traffic.

"Are you heading some place right now?"

I shrugged. "I'm always heading some place. But

nothing pressing. Just back to my room to work on a project and write up some clinical reports."

"Want to grab some coffee? I'm between classes. It's not as good as Beans, but at least it's caffeine."

I hesitated. My social life had been non-existent for the last ten weeks, mostly because I didn't want to chance running into Liam any place. Hanging with his roommate seemed like a risky proposition, but at the same time, I didn't want to hurt Giff.

"Sure."

We stood in line to order and then waited off to the side of the coffee lounge until our drinks were ready.

"No espresso?" Giff raised his eyebrows at me.

"Not here. They do basic okay, but I don't trust them with anything complicated." I held up my iced latte. "Plus it's finally getting warmer. I can drink it cold."

We threaded our way to the wall of windows at the back of the room and found a small round table for two. Giff angled his chair so that his long legs could stretch to the side.

"So tell me what's been going in your life. I haven't seen you since your birthday party."

No, he hadn't. Probably because I'd been in hiding that long.

"Absolutely nothing. Like I told you, just academics and RA shit. I live a boring existence."

"I doubt that." Giff tested his coffee and made a face. "I can't imagine Jules letting you get away with being a hermit."

I glanced away, looking out the window and smothering a sigh. But Giff didn't miss anything. "Uh-oh, what's going on? Not roommate drama, I hope? You and Julia always seemed so close."

"No drama." I shook my head. "You know I love her.

And Jesse is awesome. But she's just never around anymore. Even when she was dating—" I couldn't bring myself to say his name. "Um, dating before, she at least came back to the dorm every night. And we still hung out a lot. But now she's practically living over at Jesse's house. I'm happy for her, really I am, but sometimes it's ...lonely."

"Well, we can't let that go on. It just so happens that today is your lucky day."

I smiled. Giff was one of the most caring, compassionate people I knew. Just a shame he lived with a dickhead.

"Oh, really? Why is that?"

"Because Jeff and I are throwing a big welcome-back-spring party tonight. He's got a townhouse off campus, and we're going to put some sausage and burgers on his grill, buy some potato salad ...a bunch of the guys went in on a keg and for those of us with more refined tastes, we'll have wine. It's Friday night, winter's over and it's time to celebrate. Be there by seven."

It was so tempting. The idea of hanging out with Giff and his boyfriend and eating summertime food sounded so much better than having leftover Chinese takeout in my silent dorm. But there was one big reason not to go, and I couldn't even ask Giff if his roommate was going to be there. No one knew about Liam and me except for Julia ...and she didn't have the full story.

"I don't know, Giff. I really need to stay focused. There's only another eight weeks left before finals. And I'm trying to get an internship here this summer."

"Awesome, but taking one night to let off some steam and just kick back isn't going to kill you." He reached across the table to cover my hand with his. "Remember, peaches, I'm in the same boat as you. No rich daddy is paying my bills. I'm looking for a job, too, so I can stay

with Jeff and not have to spend the summer back in Po-
dunk."

I laughed. "Peaches, huh ...why do you call me that?"

He cocked his head and gave me that irresistible Giff
grin. "Yep. You're sitting there in the sunlight, with that
peaches-and-cream skin my mom used to talk about ...so
you're peaches. And you're coming tonight. Plan on it, or
you'll break my heart."

"Giff, you're crazy. Break your heart. Sure." I shook
my head, trying not to remember Liam touching my
breast, saying my skin was like milk. Or the warm white
sand on a beach.

"I'm a hundred percent serious. If you're not there at
seven, I'll send Liam over to drag your ass to Jeff's. That's
not a threat, it's a promise."

My breath caught, and my face must have shown apprehension, because Giff narrowed his eyes. "What's that
all about? Since when are you afraid of Liam?"

I managed a laugh. "Afraid? Don't be ridiculous. I
just don't like the idea of being dragged anywhere. And
you know after what happened with Jules and Liam ..."

"That's water under the bridge. Julia's okay with him.
Why wouldn't you be?"

"I don't know what you're talking about." I tilted my
cup back, letting the last bits of coffee drizzle into my
mouth.

"Then prove it. Here." He pulled out his phone and
typed something into it, and then mine buzzed. "I just sent
you Jeff's address. Oh, and invite Jules and her lover boy,
too. Everyone's welcome."

"They're going to a Phillies game tonight."

"So there's absolutely no reason you can't come
over." He glanced down at the phone. "I've got to mam-
bo. Class in five." He stood up, slung his bag over his

shoulder and pointed at me. "I'll see you tonight. Be there or beware." He winked, laughing at his own word play and left.

I dropped my forehead into my hands. Great. Now what?

BY FIVE O'CLOCK, I had worked myself into what my mom would have called a tizzy. I tried to concentrate on finishing the documentation for my History and Systems of Psychology research paper, but the voices in my mind would not shut up.

If I don't go, Giff is going to figure it's because of Liam.

Giff won't even notice if I'm not there.

Maybe if Giff tells Liam he invited me, Liam won't show up.

And then Giff will be even more suspicious.

What does it matter if Giff figures it out? It's over. Liam Bailey was a momentary aberration in my life.

I had just decided that I wasn't going to the party when my phone signaled an incoming text. It was from Julia.

Giff says you're going to a party tonight. YAY! Have fun.

I stuck out my tongue at the screen. Stupid Giff and his meddling ways.

I don't know if I'm going. He invited me.

It only took a moment before she replied.

Why wouldn't you go? And don't say you have home-

work. You just told me last night that you're ahead in everything.

I could have kicked myself for telling her that.

It's Friday night. You know how crazy the girls get. I need to stay close.

As arguments went, it was weak. I'd never let being an RA keep me from doing whatever I wanted. Granted, my social life had always been laughable, but Jules and I had gone to the movies or dinner on many a Friday night. She was going to call me on it.

Bullshit. Most of them will be out, too. GO.

I decided if I just stopped answering her, she'd have to give up.

I was wrong.

Ava, if you don't promise me right now that you're going, I'm telling Jesse I can't go with him to the game tonight. I'll drive home, and I will drag you over there. And then you'll have pissed off Jesse, me, and the Phillies because you know they can't win if I'm not watching.

I groaned. What was wrong with these people? Couldn't they just leave me alone to live my sad, pathetic, lonely life? I picked up my phone again and pounded in my answer.

Fine. Whatever. I'll go. But I'm not staying long. And I won't have fun, because I'm only doing this so you and Giff will leave me the hell alone.

I stomped over to my closet, pausing when I heard another text come in.

That's my girl. Can't wait to hear about it. Love you, Ave.

"Sure you do, That's why you're making me nuts." I stumbled over a pair of Julia's strappy high-heeled shoes that she'd left in the middle of the floor. Picking one of them up, I threw it hard against the wall. It gave me a little bit of satisfaction.

I was tempted to wear the same jeans and t-shirt I'd had on all day, just to show that I really didn't care and didn't want to go to this party. But then I thought of Giff. I didn't want to hurt his feelings by acting like a spoiled brat who didn't get her own way. It wouldn't hurt to look good. And if Liam were there, making him eat his heart out wouldn't bother me a bit. Why it mattered was something I didn't care to think about.

I dug out the flouncy little black jersey skirt I'd bought on sale last fall. I'd only worn it once, to a party at Alpha Delt a few months ago. That night I'd paired it with a slouchy gray sweater, but now it was too warm for that choice. I flipped hangers until I found one of my favorite green tank tops. I wriggled out of my jeans and pulled the tee over my head, and then changed my bra for one with a deeper plunge between the cups. The skirt made my short legs look longer than they were, and the tank's scoop neck showed off my deep cleavage. I smiled with satisfaction, remembering what Antonia used to say.

"God gave us great boobs to make up for how short and stumpy we are."

I'd worn my hair up in a ponytail all day, so I let it down and brushed out the snarls. No sense in curling it if we were going to be outside anyway. But I gave in to vanity and touched up my make-up a little, adding some more blush, another sweep of black mascara and some lip gloss.

My phone buzzed twice in close succession. I sighed and flipped it over.

Take a picture so I can see what you're wearing.

I stood in front of the mirror and snapped a photo, then sent it to Julia.

Why, don't you trust me? And shouldn't you be on your way to the game?

Ooooooh, hot mama! Smokin'. No, I don't trust you. Yes, we're on the bridge.

I smiled and flipped to the other message. It was from Giff.

I hope you're dressed and ready. You should be heading over here. Don't make me send out the cavalry.

Good golly, these people needed to get their own lives.

I'm leaving in a minute. Thanks for tattling on me to Julia.

See you in a few, peaches.

J EFF LIVED A few miles off campus in a part of town that was just beginning to expand. The complex had a new feel to it, with pristine white wooden siding and dark wood doors and shutters. As I turned into the parking lot, I had the unsettling sense of feeling like I didn't belong here. Having a party at a real house instead of a dorm or even on-campus apartment felt oddly grown-up. I wasn't sure I was quite ready yet.

I smelled the grill before I saw the crowd of people standing outside a corner unit. Giff waved to me and pointed to an open spot across the lot. I swung in, turned off the car and sat for a minute, just getting up the nerve to open the door.

A knock on the window made me jump. Giff stood there, looking down at me with his eyebrows raised. I reached for the handle as he stepped to the side.

"What are you doing, sitting out here? You do know we don't provide car service, right? You actually have to get out, come over and socialize?"

I glanced up at him, and he must have seen the dread in my eyes, because his voice softened.

"C'mon, peaches. I know Jules and I pushed you to come tonight, but it's because we love you, and we don't want you hiding. I get that it's scary to go into a new situation all by yourself." He extended his hand. "But you're not alone. I'm here for you."

I took a deep breath and laid my hand in his. He gave it a squeeze and pulled me to my feet. His eyes widened in approval as he took in my outfit, and he whistled.

"Look at you! Sometimes I forget what a beauty you are under the jeans and sweatshirts."

"Thanks, Giff. You sure know how to make a girl feel special."

"It's a gift."

We walked across the black top, and Giff led me to the grill, where Jeff and another guy I didn't recognize were flipping burgers and drinking beer. I had only met Jeff once before, but he greeted me with a big bear hug.

"Hey, Ava! I'm glad you could make it." He waved the spatula in the direction of the other man. "This is Drew."

I smiled as Drew gave me a wave. Jeff lowered the lid on the grill and held up his clear plastic cup.

"Want a beer?"

Before I could answer, Giff slung his arm over my shoulder. "Nope, Ava's a wine girl. I'm taking her inside to show her around, and I'll get her set up."

"Cool. Come on back out when you're done."

I followed Giff around the side of the building, past the keg, to a deck off the back. A group of girls stood near one side, chatting. I knew they were from Birch, but I didn't know them by name. Giff made a few introduction as my stomach flipped and tightened. A party girl I was not. Meeting new people like this stressed me out.

We moved into the kitchen, which was blessedly empty. The table was covered with bottles of wine, soda and liquors of just about every variety.

"And here we have the bar. What can I pour for you? White wine or red?"

I hesitated. Wine was the safe-Ava choice, something I could sip on for a while and then be able to drive home at the end of the night. But I was jittery in this house full of people I didn't know, and suddenly I needed a little bit of liquid courage.

"Umm ...no. Something stronger. With—" I cast my eyes over the selection. "Vodka."

Giff grinned. "Okay then, you wild woman. How about a screwdriver?"

"Sure." Whatever that was. It sounded familiar; Julia might have drunk those once or twice.

He opened the fridge to get the orange juice. "Drew's a decent guy. He just moved down here from Trenton. He's a cop."

"Oh, yeah?" I watched him shake up the juice, pour into a plastic cup and add a healthy slug of vodka. "Should I ask how you met him?"

"Ha." Giff added ice and handed me the cup. "Salut, my friend. No, he lives three doors down. But he doesn't know anyone around here, and he's only about a year older than us. So Jeff thought it would be nice if he met some people tonight." He looked at me meaningfully.

"Thanks, but no thanks. I'm not looking to get matched up, Giff."

He sighed, heavy on the dramatics. "I know, it goes against the master plan. But you don't have to marry the guy, Ave. Just talk to him. You might find out you have something in common, and at least maybe you'd get out once a month to have a cup of coffee with a real live person."

I took an experimental sip of the drink. It was good. I could taste the vodka, but it wasn't overwhelming. I drank a little more, and then drained the cup.

"This is delicious. Thanks."

"Whoa there, kiddo. That's strong stuff. Slow down."

I shook my head. "C'mon, Giff. Make me another one. I'm Italian, I can handle it."

"Okay, okay. You're strong, I get it." He replenished the juice and didn't skimp on the vodka. "Here you are. Drink up, and then go talk to Drew. Get your flirt on, peaches."

This screwdriver packed a bigger punch than the first one had. I downed half of it, smiled and cocked my eyebrow. "Did you ever think I might be looking for more than just a flirt?"

Giff leered. "Oooh, baby. I must have made that drink stronger than I thought. Well, go for it. It'd be good for you to go a little wild."

I raised my cup in a toast, feeling a little buzzed already. "That's why I'm here, right?" I meant the words to sound ironic, but they may have been just a little slurred.

"Exactly my point. You need to—" He broke off, looking over my shoulder. "Hey, Liam. I was wondering when you were going to get here."

My heart sped up, and I felt like the kitchen floor had tilted. I could feel him behind me, his eyes on me, but I was too chicken to turn around. I froze like a statue and kept my eyes on Giff.

From the way he was looking from one of us to the other, I figured Liam must have been shocked to see me there. I could imagine the expression on his face all too well. Giff frowned at me as he picked up his cup of wine.

"Can I get you something to drink?" He pointed to the table, watching Liam.

"No, thanks. I'll take care of it."

"Cool. Then one of you want to tell me what the hell is going on between you? The air just got real thick in here."

I couldn't speak yet, but I lifted one shoulder in a shrug. I felt prickles down the back of my neck as though his fingers were walking down my spine, and I wanted to turn toward him. I wanted to forget everything that I had said or feared or suspected and just let him wrap me in his arms.

"Leave it alone, Giff." The tone of Liam's voice made it clear that he didn't want any argument.

"Uh, maybe you've forgotten who you're talking to, beetle. Leaving shit alone isn't exactly in my personality." Giff smirked, and he opened his mouth as though to say more. He was interrupted by the door opening as one of the girls from the deck leaned in.

"Giff, Jeff says he needs those platters. Can you bring them out?"

"Sure, be right there." Taking a long gulp of wine, he pointed first to me and then to the doorway where I assumed Liam still stood. "You two ...don't think this is over. I'll be back."

He snagged two large plates off the counter and swung out the door. I sagged against the table in front of me, pulling out a chair so I could sit down. I heard Liam's footsteps coming closer, but I didn't look up.

He reached over me to pluck a cup from the pile, and then he grabbed bottle of whiskey and poured a generous slug. I tried not to see his hands or inhale his scent, but it was impossible and all too tempting. I did manage to keep from checking out the way his jeans fit his ass, and I didn't let my mind meander back to how the zipper had looked when his erection was straining against it.

"Shit." I breathed out the word, closed my eyes and slumped in the chair, dropping my head against my folded arms.

"Problem?" The one word held a combination of weariness and caution that made me want to cry. He didn't trust me, and I couldn't blame him.

"I'm sorry I'm here." My voice was muffled in my elbow. "I didn't want to come. But Giff insisted. And then Julia ...anyway. I'll go. I don't belong here anyway."

Liam threw back the whiskey. "Don't leave on my account. I can go to the front, and you can stay here. Or hang out on the deck. I wouldn't want to stop you from— what was it you were saying to Giff? You're here to have a wild time?"

I flushed as I sat up. "I was joking. Giff was pushing me to meet the policeman—Jeff's neighbor—oh, why the hell am I bothering?" I stood, pushing against the table, and I tossed back the last of my screwdriver. The vodka hit my stomach and zipped through my blood, giving me the courage to finally look at Liam.

It was a mistake. Seeing him, meeting his eyes, was more intoxicating than the liquor. His hair was a little longer than I was used to, falling in tousled waves over his ears and forehead. His bright blue eyes, usually so intense and serious, were tired. I twined my fingers together to keep from reaching toward him to brush over his face.

The fact that he was gazing right back at me didn't make it any easier. Not with longing or hunger, as he had once, but with a guarded sort of interest. Remembering our last conversation, I couldn't blame him. I reminded myself that I had had a reason for what I'd done. At the time, it had felt like the only way to get my life back, to have control again. Looking back through the lens of two lonely months, during which I had had an endless supply of empty hours to think about it, I wasn't so sure.

"Did you really come here tonight to hook up with someone?" Liam poured another drink.

Had I? That didn't sound like me, but then again, everything was feeling a little less than clear right now.

"I just didn't want to be alone." The truth poured out without me intending. "For once, I wanted to be with people and not think." I picked up the orange juice Giff had left on the table and splashed a little into my empty cup and then surveyed the other bottles, trying to find the vodka. Unscrewing the bottle took a little more coordination than I had at the moment, but I finally got it open and added it to the OJ until the liquid skimmed the top of the cup.

"Whoa. Maybe you should slow down a little on that." Liam's hand closed over the bottle, not quite touching mine.

"Maybe you should mind your own damn business and leave me alone." I raised the drink to my mouth and took a long sip, never dropping my eyes from Liam's, daring him to say anything else.

"I thought you didn't want to be alone. Isn't that why you're here?"

I shook back my hair out of my face. "I don't remember." This drink didn't taste as good as the one Giff had made me, but when it came to making me feel braver, more daring, it did the trick. I tilted the cup back, using my tongue to hold the ice from hitting me.

"Not remembering is a sign that you've probably had enough to drink. Come on, let's go outside and see if the food's ready. I bet you don't have anything in your stomach but vodka."

"You'd be wrong." I stabbed a finger at him, which was no easy feat since I swaying on my feet. "There's orange juice, too."

"Sorry, my mistake." Liam came around the table toward me, and my heart sped up. I knew I should duck away, but I didn't want to do it. I had a sudden vision of him running his finger under the edge of my dress as we lay in my bed, and the memory made my face burn. The rest of me wasn't far behind.

I thought he might pull me against his body, but he didn't. Instead, he took hold of my upper arm and steered me toward the door that led to the deck. I didn't have any choice but to stumble along.

The door slammed shut behind us, and Liam stopped in front of vacant lounge. He nudged at my knees until they bent and I fell back into the chair.

"Stay here." He wheeled around, heading for the steps, and then turned back glare at me. "And no more to drink."

"I couldn't if I wanted to. You left my cup inside." I pouted, crossing my arms over my chest. Of course, I could just get up and go get my drink if I really wanted it. But the kitchen door looked strangely far away. The idea of standing and walking seemed like too much work. I scooted back along the webbing of the lounge and dropped my head onto the built-in pillow. It felt good to be almost lying down, even if the damn deck was spinning.

"Liam's pushy, huh?" I opened one eye to see a girl leaning against the deck railing.

I laughed, one short bark. "You have no idea."

"Maybe I do. I've known him since high school. I was a year behind him and Giff."

Now she had my interest. "Really? Has he always been this much of a dick?"

My new friend laughed, throwing back her head. She was tall, pretty in a careless way. Her dark hair had streaks of red in it and was piled on the top of her head in a messy bun. I was pretty sure she wasn't wearing any makeup, and her jeans were worn. Still, she had that same look I'd noticed in other girls from Birch: even when they dressed down, there was an air of panache and style that came from having money. Her jeans might have had holes in the knee, but I was pretty sure they cost more than I paid for my entire wardrobe.

She was holding a clear plastic cup with some kind red liquid in it, and she shook the ice, rattling it before she answered me.

"Liam's okay. I didn't know he was dating anyone, though. How long have you guys been going out?"

"Me and Liam?" I shook my head. "No. We're ...I just know him. A little."

She cocked her head at me. "Didn't look like that to me. The way he was looking at you—well, I should mind my own business."

I didn't want her to stop talking. I wanted to hear more about how Liam was looking at me, even if I didn't believe it. I needed to stop thinking.

"What's that you're drinking?" I pointed at her cup.

"This? Oh, just jungle juice."

"Is it good?"

She smirked. "Yeah, I guess you could say that. Here, I only had a sip. You can have it."

I took the cup, careful not to let it spill. Red punch was a bitch to get out of clothes. My first impression was that this drink was much sweeter than the orange juice I'd been having. And then it hit me with a punch as the alcohol burned down my throat.

"Amanda, what the hell?"

I looked up to where Liam was standing behind my benefactor. He held two plates of food. Or maybe just one. It was hard to tell because focusing my eyes was becoming an issue.

Amanda grinned at him. "What? Your girlfriend wanted to try my drink. I was just sharing."

"Jungle juice? Are you crazy?" He set one plate on the railing and reached for my cup. I held it away.

"Stop. What are you doing?" My voice sounded like I was a two year-old trying to hold onto her favorite toy.

"Trying to save you from a world of pain. Give me that."

"No." I took another big swallow, just to spite him.

"Ava, for God's sake. Stop. You're being stupid. Look, I brought you food."

"I'm not hungry." That wasn't strictly true. The smell of the burgers made my mouth water.

"I don't care. You need to eat something. Here, let me hold your cup and you take the plate."

"You just want to take away my drink."

"Why don't I hold it for you while you eat?" Amanda came to my rescue. I knew I could trust her, so I handed my cup over. Liam sighed as he set the plate in my lap. A plastic fork and knife lay across the side, but for the life of me, I couldn't quite figure out how to use them. I decided to stick to the burger that I could just pick up and bite.

100

Liam dragged a chair over to sit near me and dug into his own plate. The silence as we ate while Amanda stood near us felt awkward, so I spoke up.

"Amanda says she went to high school with you and Giff."

Liam glanced up. "Yeah. She did."

I narrowed my eyes as I chewed. "So did you two ..." I used my free hand to point at them, one and then the other. "You know. Did you ever get together?"

Amanda's hoot of laughter startled me, and Liam just shook his head.

"What? What's so funny?" I looked at them in confusion.

"Nothing." Liam rolled his eyes. "It's just that I've known Amanda for a long time. We kind of grew up like brother and sister. Her mother is in politics, too."

"Oh, tell her the truth." Amanda was drinking my jungle juice, but I decided since it had been hers in the first place, I couldn't object. "He tried to kiss me once, when we were freshmen in high school. We were in the pool at my house, and I laughed so hard at him, I almost drowned."

"Did you *like* her?" I demanded, staring at Liam.

He rolled his eyes. "This might be the most bizarre conversation I've ever had."

Amanda poked him in the ribs. "What's wrong, Liam? You don't want to explain our sordid past to your girlfriend?"

"I'm not his girlfriend." My voice carried more than I expected, and several other people on the deck turned to look at us.

"No. She's not my girlfriend." Liam sounded tired again.

"Who isn't whose girlfriend?" Giff appeared behind

Amanda, wrapping one arm around her shoulders.

"This girl—I'm sorry, I didn't get your name. She isn't Liam's girlfriend. Even though he tells her what she can and cannot drink, and brings her plates of food."

A broad grin split Giff's face. "I didn't know that was even a question. Fascinating what you learn about your friends. And sorry, Amanda, Liam's rude. This is Ava. She goes to Birch with us."

"Don't you go to Birch, too?" I had the feeling I'd missed something.

"No, I go to U of Penn. I'm just over here for the weekend to see Giff."

"Huh." I nodded. "Nice to meet you. Thanks for sharing your drink."

"No problem. So if you're not his girlfriend, what's going on with the two of you?"

This Amanda chick was blunt. Giff was looking down at me over her shoulder, his eyes bright and curious.

"Yes, do tell. Inquiring minds want to know. What *is* going on with the two of you, and why the hell didn't I know anything about it?"

I turned to face Amanda. "Liam dated my roommate for a year. That's how I got to know him and Giff. That's it."

"*Almost* a year," Liam corrected. "And ..." His eyes heated as they raked down me. "Yeah. That's it."

"It's not. You're both hiding something, but whatever. Live and let live, it's what I always say." Giff shot me a look that said this wasn't over. Luckily I was too cocooned in a cloud of vodka and jungle juice to care.

"I'm going to find some food." Amanda pushed off the railing and bumped her shoulder into Giff's. "Let's go get your stud muffin to make me a well-done burger, okay? Come on."

I watched them go down the steps onto the grass, all of a sudden very aware of Liam sitting next to me. He had finished eating and was folding his paper plate in half.

My tongue darted out to moisten my bottom lip. The sun had set, and the deck was in shadows. Everyone but us had moved down to the yard, giving the illusion of privacy.

"Was your food good?" Liam's voice was husky. I swore I could feel it everywhere, on the tips of my breasts and down between my legs. Getting drunk made me horny. Or maybe I'd drunk too much because I was horny?

"Yeah." I cleared my throat, but I couldn't seem to manage more than a squeak. "Thanks for getting it for me."

"You're welcome." He leaned back in the chair, stretching his legs so that they went under my lounge, running beneath my hips. I remember lying on his lap, snuggled against him, slipping off to sleep. My breath caught and shuddered. I clenched my hands into fists because he was so close to me that I could have reached out to touch his thigh. I could have run my fingers up to his flat stomach and slid them into his jeans ...

"My God." I closed my eyes and gripped my legs together, trying to quell the ache there in my center.

"What?" Liam sounded curious.

"Nothing." I couldn't move or I was fairly certain that I'd climb over and straddle him. Assuming I could do that without falling; the world was still a little spinny. I tried to think of something else to say, anything to get my mind off Liam's body.

"Why did Giff call you beetle? Back in the kitchen, I mean."

He chuckled. "You know Giff and his nicknames. When we were in high school, he started calling me that.

You know, like the comic strip? Beetle Bailey?"

"Beetle Bailey." I giggled. It was so much funnier to me that it should have been.

I heard the creak as he shifted in his chair. "You look amazing tonight, by the way."

"You can't say that."

"Really? Why?" He was laughing at me, but I didn't care.

"Because. What happened with us. What I did. What you did."

"What I did? Just what am I supposed to have done?"

I turned my head in his direction and opened my eyes, not saying anything.

Liam held up a hand. "Okay, I'll concede to the shit that went down with Julia. What did I do to you?"

I closed my eyes again. "You made me think ...maybe I could have something I'm not supposed to have." Even drunk, listening to my own slurring words, I recognized convoluted logic. It made sense in my head, but out loud ...not so much.

When Liam spoke again, his voice was much closer to my ear. "Why are you not supposed to have it?"

I let my eyelids flutter open, and I stared into those heart-stopping blue eyes. "Because bad things happen when I do. I have to be the good girl. I have to focus. Eyes on the prize."

"Ah." He didn't argue, and I was glad. I wasn't sure I could remember anything else. "So now we know what I did. What did you do that makes it so I can't tell you how sexy you look?"

Desire made me writhe. "Stop it. Don't say that." I forced myself not to look away. "I said hurtful things. I made you think it was all a game. You and me. I wanted to make you go away, so I could get my life back. My lonely,

104

boring life."

I expected Liam to sit back. He should have been pissed at what I'd just revealed, but he didn't move. His gaze ran down my face, fastening on my lips, and then back to my eyes. Before I could react, he shifted a fraction of an inch forward to touch his lips to mine.

It was a tentative kiss, just the barest meeting of lips. He kept still for several heartbeats, as though he were waiting for my reaction. When I leaned back, angling my head to capture his mouth, he grunted deep in his throat and moved one hand up to hold my face. All hesitation was gone; he devoured me as his lips moved with purpose and his tongue stroked me, running over the inside of my lips and then plunging hard to engage mine.

I was laid out, open, and completely given in. I don't know what would have happened if a different sort of urgency hadn't gripped me.

"Stop." I flattened my hands on Liam's chest, pushing when he would have ignored me. "Move. You need to move."

"Why?" He rested his forehead against mine.

I rolled out from under him, struggled off the lounge chair and lunged for the far side of the deck, as far away from people as I could get.

And then I leaned over the railing and proceeded to puke, loud and long.

Ch♥pter Eight

DEATH. OH, PLEASE, just a little death right now. Anything to stop the pain.

"Good morning, peaches."

I moaned and pulled the pillow over my head. "Shut up. Shut up, shut up, shut up."

"Sorry, darling. It's nearly noon, and your roommate is frantic. She's been texting me for hours, afraid you were in a hospital in a coma or worse. You need to let Jules know you're still among the living."

"I'm not sure I am. And if I am, I don't want to be."

"You don't get that choice. Come on. Up and at 'em."

I ventured to open one eye. "Where am I?"

"Jeff's guest room."

I blew out an unsteady breath. "Oh, my God. He must think I'm such an idiot. I'm so sorry, Giff."

"Nothing to be worried about, sweetness. We've all had nights like that." I felt the bed dip as he sat down next to me. "But maybe you'd like to talk about the whys and wherefores."

"Does it matter? It's over. I just want to forget last

night ever happened. And maybe die."

"Hmm. I don't think we can make either of those things happen. Pretty sure you're going to live. And it just so happens that Liam is sitting downstairs in the kitchen, eating breakfast with Jeff and Amanda."

"Giff." I pushed to sit up and then clutched at my middle. "Shit. Oh, my God." Pain seized my stomach, and nausea danced in my throat. I stayed still until I could speak again. "I can't see Liam. I'll just go out the back way ..." I trailed off, remembering the layout of the house. "Or the front way. Don't say anything. Just let me go."

"Ava, you can't run forever. I don't know for sure what happened between you and Liam, but judging from what you said last night while under the influence and a few things I picked up from Liam, I can guess. Both of you screwed up, I get it, but why don't you talk to him? Maybe work out whatever wacky thing the two of you have going?"

I shoved a pillow behind my back and gingerly leaned against it. "It's complicated, Giff."

He raised his eyebrows. "Funny, that's the same line Liam gave me. Maybe the two of you need to figure out how to simplify it."

I shook my head and then regretted it as the pain reverberated in my brain.

Giff stood up. "It's up to you, Ava. Your clothes are on the dresser over there. And don't worry, your virtue is intact. Amanda's the one who helped you get changed and lent you that t-shirt. So while you're deciding whether you're going to sneak away or face the music, you should remember you owe her a thank you. She also gave you her bed, since she was supposed to have the guest room last night."

He flashed me a meaningful glance before he left,

closing the door behind him.

"This. This is what happens when I step off the path."
I flipped the covers off and attempted to stand. "Oh, God.
I think I'm going to become a nun."

"That would be a shame."

Liam stood in the doorway, leaning against the jam,
watching me with a smirk. He was looking decidedly
rumpled, and he needed a shave. The messed-up hair and
morning scruff only made me want him more.

His eyes widened as they wandered down my body,
and I remembered that I had on only a t-shirt that skimmed
the top of my thighs and a tiny wisp of panties beneath.
My legs were bare, and my boobs were unfettered. Never a good idea. I crossed my arms over my chest and sat
down on the bed again, tugging a blanket over my legs.

"What are you doing here?"

Liam strolled into the room as though it were the
most natural thing in the world. He closed the door behind
him and sat on the other side of the bed.

"I'm not sure what you mean. I'm still here from last
night, because I'd had too much to drink to drive back to
campus. Plus, I was worried about you. I'm still here for
breakfast because Jeff makes a mean waffle. And I wanted
to talk to you."

"I'm sorry about last night. I'm ...mortified. I never
act like that."

He leaned as though to touch me but stopped short.
"You don't have to be embarrassed. We've all been there.
The worst thing you did was puke in the bushes."

"No, it's not. I said things, and I ..." I cast down my
eyes, staring at my own bare feet. "I kissed you."

"I was a little drunk, too, but I'm pretty sure I kissed
you first. And Ava, why is that such a big deal? It's not like
it's the first time."

I wanted to stamp my foot in frustration, but being short meant that my legs dangled over the side of the bed without reaching the floor. I had to settle for punching the pillow. It didn't have the same effect.

"It doesn't matter if it was the first time or the fiftieth. It's wrong, I shouldn't have done it, and I ...won't do it again. I was stupid to come here last night."

"Why did you?" I heard the curiosity tinge his words, taking away any sting they might have had.

I toyed with the edge of the bedspread. "I don't know. Giff and Jules both pestered me about it, but I could've said no." I shrugged. "Julia's been spending most of her time with Jesse. I was tired of nights in the room by myself, and when they pushed, I let them." I bit down on the corner of my lip. "I'm sorry."

"Stop apologizing. And please tell me you weren't serious about becoming a nun. It would be a real waste ...of your assets." He grinned at me.

"Don't worry. No convent would take me." I said it so glumly that Liam laughed.

"That's probably not a bad thing."

"It would be in my family. None of my brothers or my sister went into the Church, so my mom would probably be thrilled if I did." I cocked my head, considering. "I wouldn't be lonely at least."

Liam stretched out on the bed, lying on his side. "That's kind of an extreme plan to avoid being alone. You could maybe try something a little less drastic, like, say ...going out with me."

I groaned and fell into the pillow. "Liam, please. I'm barely holding it together right now. I've never had a hangover like this. I'm not sure I can stand up. Don't tease me."

"Yeah, that jungle juice is lethal. Some of the guys

call it a punch in the balls, because the next day, you'd rather have a punch there than feel like you do." He flipped a strand of hair out of my face. "I guess that doesn't mean much to you."

"Not really. But I have a good imagination."

"Hey, I did warn you. That stuff eats through the plastic cups if you leave it long enough. And by the way, I wasn't teasing you. About going out with me."

I peeked out at him from the pillow. "We've been through this, Liam. Nothing has changed for me. I'm not the dating kind of girl."

If I though he might argue that point, I would have been disappointed. He let his eyes drift closed for a moment, and I saw his throat work as he swallowed.

"How about a friend kind of girl? Are you that?"

"What's that supposed to mean?"

"You said you've been lonely. You could use a friend. Why not me?"

I bent my arm and tucked it under my head. "I can think of about a million reasons. Starting with, why would you want to be my friend? I haven't been very pleasant to be around."

"Yeah, well, I'm not exactly prince charming myself. Maybe we're a good pair. Of friends," he added when I raised one eyebrow at him.

"What does friendship mean? With you, specifically."

He rolled over onto his back. "I think the rules would be open to interpretation. Maybe we can make them up as we go along."

"Hmm." I pulled the blanket up a little higher over my chest. "I'm not sure that's a good idea. We should at least have some basic guidelines."

A little smile played on his lips. "Of course we should. And they would be?"

I held up my fingers, ticking them off one at a time. "No kissing. No touching. No holding my hand. No saying suggestive things."

"Hold on, clarification needed." He put up his palm like a stop sign. "That whole suggestive thing is very subjective. What I think is a perfectly innocent comment might be against the rules if someone takes it the wrong way."

"Use your best judgment."

A buzzing sounded somewhere in the room. I glanced over to the dresser, where my skirt and top from last night were still folded. The little purse with my phone in it lay next to the clothes, and it was shaking.

"Shit!" Without thinking, I jumped out of bed to get the phone. I missed the call, but to my relief, it was only Julia. I typed her a quick message that I was fine and would be on my way back to the dorm in a few minutes.

"You know, this is one of those situations that feels like a gray area. I mean, as your friend, is staring at your ass creepy, or is it kind of like a compliment?"

"God, Liam." I wrapped the end of the sheet around the lower half of my body. "I need to get dressed. Can you go back downstairs, please?"

"So I guess that's a yes on the creepy. Good to know." He stretched and stood up. "Stop in the kitchen on your way out. Jeff made you something for your head and stomach. Not a cure, but it should help."

COLLEGE WAS A time of new experiences, and one I had never had before was the walk of shame, returning home the next day in the same clothes I'd worn the night before. Until today, that is.

Amanda had offered to lend me something of hers to wear.

"I know it'll be too big for you, but you're welcome to anything in my bag."

"Thanks, but I already took your bed last night. I'll be okay. I'm going right back to the dorm."

"Here." Jeff handed me a glass of something that looked thick and green. "Drink this before you go."

"Really? But the coffee actually smells good." I glanced hopefully at the pot on the counter.

"This first, then you can have coffee. Trust me, you won't be sorry."

They all watched me as I sipped the glass suspiciously. To my shock, it was good. There was a fruity taste, and the ice-cold texture soothed my throat. I smiled thanks at Jeff.

"Liam's going to drive you home in your car, and I'll follow in his," Giff told me.

"Oh, you don't have to do that. I'm fine to drive." I pushed the empty glass away.

"Not up for discussion." Liam stood and handed his keys to Giff. "Thanks again for breakfast, Jeff. And for the party."

"Any time, man." Jeff leaned back in his chair. "See you tonight, Giff?"

"You know it." Giff leaned down to kiss him.

I scraped back my chair. "Jeff, I'm sorry about last night. We don't know each other very well, but trust me, that was not normal behavior for me."

He pulled me into a warm hug. "No worries. We've all been there. Some of us more often than others. I'm glad you came over last night. Don't be a stranger, okay?"

I nodded and managed a smile.

Amanda grinned at me over her coffee. "I'm sure I'll see you around, Ava. Get these guys to bring you into the city, and I'll show you how we party there."

Grimacing, I shook my head. "Not sure I'm ready to think about drinking again yet, but thanks. For everything."

Liam held the door as we went out, and then opened his hand to me as we walked across the parking lot. "Keys?"

I unzipped my purse. "Liam, I appreciate the offer, but really, I'm okay to drive. The stuff Jeff made me helped."

He wriggled his fingers without answering. With an exasperated sigh, I dropped the keys into his palm. He closed his fingers around my hand, holding tight for a minute before releasing.

"What was that?" I climbed into the passenger seat and fastened my seat belt.

"What was what?" Liam had adopted an air of innocence.

"You held my hand. That's against the rules."

"Oh, yeah. Sorry. Hand spasm." He winked at me as he turned the key in the ignition.

I rolled my eyes. "You know, there's something I don't understand. I know what I get out of this friendship deal. But what about you? You're not exactly lacking for company."

He didn't look away from the road. "There's company, and then there's company. I know a lot of people. But that doesn't mean I can talk to them. Feel comfortable with them."

"What about Giff?"

"He's cool. But he's busy with Jeff now. See, we're in the same boat. Our roommates found true love, and we're left out. It makes sense."

"Hmmm." I wasn't sure I bought that rationale. "Is everything okay with you? I thought last night you looked a little tired."

He pretended I'd offended him. "Thanks a lot."

"You know what I mean."

He was silent for long enough that I thought he'd decided not to answer. "Stuff going on with my parents. It's ...you know how that is. Or maybe you don't. You get along pretty well with your family, don't you?"

I thought of the tiny home where I'd grown up, and the noise level on Sunday afternoons. Loud, crazy, but always full of love.

"Yeah. They make me nuts sometimes, but I love them."

"Count yourself lucky." His jaw tightened. "Mine have a ton of expectations, and sometimes I get the feeling that if I don't live up to them ..." He shrugged. "Let's just say I don't think my parents do unconditional love very well." He pulled into the lot adjacent to my dorm. We both got out of the car, and I turned to say good-bye and get my keys.

"I'll walk you up. Giff isn't here yet, anyway."

"Liam, do you think that's a good idea? Look at me. I'm a mess. Bad enough I have to walk through the dorm like this, in front of all my freshman girls, but if you're with me, people will think ..." I stopped talking, my point made.

"Do you care? I don't. Come on. We're just two friends, coming back after a night of partying." He began walking toward the building, leaving me to scramble to keep up with him.

"But you were so worried about Julia and what everyone was saying about her. Why doesn't it bother you that they might talk about me?"

114

"Mostly because I don't think anyone is even going to notice. People assume the best of you, Ava. You're kind of Teflon, you know?"

We climbed the steps, passing by several girls who only gave me a quick wave or smile. No one looked at me funny or pointed or stared. In fact, none of them seemed to notice. I frowned. Liam may have had a point.

I expected him to drop me at the door and leave, but he didn't show any signs of being in a hurry to go. I turned the doorknob and nearly fell inside as the door swung open.

"*There* you are!" Julia grabbed me and pulled me into a tight hug. "My God, Ava, I was so worried. I tried texting you, and you didn't answer, and I called ...I left Jesse's early to come back, and you weren't here. I was about to call the police. Or your mother."

"Oh, you wouldn't have." I clapped my hand over my heart. "You know the rule. Don't call my mom until you see my body on the slab at the morgue."

"That's dark." Liam had retreated to the background, out of Julia's way. Now she noticed him, surprise on her face.

"You don't know my mother." I smiled at Liam. "She doesn't just jump to conclusions. She leaps over tall buildings to get to them. If Jules had said she couldn't get in touch with me, Mom would have sent my brothers down and maybe called out the National Guard."

"What are you doing here?" Julia folded her arms over her chest and stared down her ex-boyfriend.

"Making sure Ava got back okay. She was still a little shaky this morning."

"Oh." Julia looked from Liam to me, her forehead drawn together.

We were all silent for a few charged beats, and then

115

Liam stepped back.

"I'm going to go. I need to get a shower, do some stuff ...I'll talk to you later, Ava." He bent to kiss my cheek before I could side-step him, then left, closing the door behind him.

Julia stood next to me, watching him go, with her mouth sagging in shock. She turned her head to look at me, eyes wide.

"Want to catch me up, Ave?"

AFTER A LONG, hot shower, I pulled on my favorite pair of yoga pants and oversized tee and climbed into bed with two textbooks. Last night had been an odd detour, but I was ready to get back on my safe and boring path.

Julia sat at her desk, working on a newspaper article. She was quiet, and more than once, I caught her gazing at me, her brows knit and her mouth tight.

Finally, after her second deep sigh, I flipped over my book and punched a pillow into shape behind me.

"Okay, what's going on, Jules? Clearly you have something on your mind. Just say it. I can't concentrate when you keep looking at me like I just got a death sentence."

"It's this thing with Liam. Are you sure you know what you're doing?"

I frowned. "What am I doing? I agreed we'd be friends. No different than what you and I both have with Giff. What's the big deal?"

Julia turned in her chair and looped her arm over the back, hooking her feet on a rung. "The big deal is that this isn't Giff, it's Liam. Giff can be our friend because he's not looking to get us into bed. Can you say the same about Liam?"

I twisted my hair into a knot. "I gave him rules. He knows what I want. And what I don't want." I tried to forget his so-called hand spasm and the casual good-bye kiss. Those were probably aberrations.

"I'm just saying, keep your eyes open. I'm not angry with Liam anymore, but I'm also not sure I trust him."

I nodded. She wasn't telling me anything I didn't know. I wasn't ready to think about it too hard. Not when I was still getting over last night. Changing the subject seemed like a good idea.

"So how was the game last night?"

Julia brightened. "So much fun. We went with a couple of Jesse's friends from grad school, and it was a great game."

"I'm glad you had a good time." I stuck my legs back under the covers. "I'm serious, you know? I'm so happy for you and Jesse."

Julia smiled, but her eyes clouded. "That sounds like there's a but at the end."

"No, no but. Maybe an and. I'm happy for you, and I need to get used to the fact that you're going to be spending more time with him. The last few months have been quiet around here for me."

"Oh, my God, Ava, I'm sorry. I didn't mean to leave you alone so much. I guess I'm just used to you being blinders-on for school, and I didn't think about making sure you didn't feel left out."

"Jules, that's not what I'm trying to say. It's just an adjustment. We've been each other's best friend since we started college, and we didn't ever have to worry about being alone. But things are bound to change. After next year, we'll be going in different directions."

Julia sniffled. "I thought we were both going to live in New York. I'm going to get a job on a prestigious weekly magazine, and you're going get into the most high-powered ad firms in the city."

I laughed. "And what I am going to do with you when the first weekend rolls around and you're missing Jesse, who's still down here finishing grad school? Face it, Jules. Our lives are changing, and they're going to keep changing. That's okay. I'm not jealous of your time with Jesse. But don't worry about me if I decide to hang out with Liam now and then."

She nodded. "Just be careful, Ave. That's all I'm saying. And if you ever feel like hanging out with Jesse and me, you know you can. Any time."

"Thanks, sweetie. But you guys are still too gooey right now. I'll wait until you can be in the same room with him without sitting in his lap."

Julia stuck her tongue out at me and turned back to the computer. My phone vibrated as I opened my book.

How are you feeling?

I smiled. It felt good to be happy about getting a message from my friend Liam, instead of stressed about getting one from Liam the guy who wanted to sleep with me.

Much better. But I'm never drinking again. Ever.

There was a pause for a minute before he replied.

Sorry, LMAO at you. Sure you won't.

Grinning, I typed my rebuttal.

Okay, I think I'll never drink anything RED ever again.

118

Probably a good policy. What are you doing tonight?

I glanced up at Julia. "Are you staying in tonight, or you going over to Jesse's?"

She didn't look away from the computer. "I'm not going anywhere. He's got some big group project to finish, and I want to get a good night's sleep."

I'm finishing up some reading and going to bed early. How about you?

There was a long pause, and I wondered if he didn't want to tell me.

I was going to see if you wanted to hang. But maybe I'll try to catch up on some homework, too.

Sounds like a good idea.

See you this week?

I sat looking down at the screen as a shot of warmth ran up my middle.

Definitely.

Ch♥pter Nine

"**A**ND IT IS finished."

I shut my laptop, rolled over onto my back and stretched. I'd been wrapped up in this research paper for Behavior Disorders for weeks, and having it done made me want to dance.

Liam turned around in the desk chair to look down at me. Without discussing it, we'd each found our own study spots when he came over to hang out with me: I spread out either on my bed or the floor, and he sat at my desk, since he didn't have the same need to sprawl that I did.

His eyes roamed down my body, and I was suddenly, uncomfortably aware that my back was arched, my breasts straining against the t-shirt that was pulled tight by my stretch. He didn't say anything that would violate the friendship rules, but I saw his mouth tighten.

I brought my knees up to my stomach, hugged them with both arms and rocked to a sitting position, wincing a little as my tailbone hit the hard tile floor beneath my throw rug.

"Do you even do yoga?" Liam raised one eyebrow as

he watched me.

"Me? Um, well, I did. Sort of. I had to take a PE class freshman year, and that's what I took."

"So are all these pants left over from that one class, three years ago?" He leaned over and pinched a piece of the stretchy material that covered my knee.

"Some are. And some I've bought since. Why?"

He grinned, shaking his head. "Because. I figured you probably were really into it, since you're always dressed like you're going to a class. It would be like me wearing a football uniform all the time and not even being on the team."

"Hey! That's not true. Yoga pants are more of a fashion choice than a work-out uniform. They're comfortable for when I'm just laying around and doing homework. And besides, I'm not *always* dressed in them. Just when I'm staying in my room."

"You wore them when we went over to Beans last week."

I gave an exaggerated sigh. "Because you said we were just going over there to grab coffee and bring it back here. And then we got there and you said you changed your mind, you wanted to stay and drink it there."

"Yeah, because we'd been cooped up here for three hours and I wanted to make sure humanity had not disappeared from the earth."

"If you had told me we were going to sit down there, I would've gotten changed into real clothes."

"No, if I'd told you I wanted to drink our coffee there, you would have whined about it and sweet-talked me into just bringing you something back to the dorm. You weren't getting out of your yoga pants either way."

I stuck out my tongue. "I don't sweet-talk you into anything. And if you don't like my yoga pants, you ..." I paused. I had been about to say, he didn't have to come study with me anymore. But I realized that wasn't what I wanted. " ...you don't have to look at me," I finished weakly.

Liam swung his legs back around to the front of the chair and stood, stretching his arms over his head so that his tight t-shirt rode up, revealing his solid abs and the teasing line of hair that disappeared into his shorts. I dropped my eyes and tried to think about anything else. Liver and onions. Jellyfish on the beach. A cold shower.

"But I like to look at you." He nudged my leg with his foot, making words that might have crossed the line to suggestive sound more like something a pal would say. "I wasn't complaining. I was just curious. You've never talked about doing anything physical."

I flashed my eyes to his face to see if he were teasing me, but he only looked interested, and not in a leering way. "What do you mean, physical? Like sports? No, I barely made it through gym class in high school. I hated it."

"No biking, dance class or tennis?" He frowned.

"Nope. We never had money for dance classes. I rode my bike when I was a kid, but then, I don't know, I just didn't have time. And tennis—" I shuddered. "Balls flying at my face are a definite no-no. Same with volleyball."

"How about badminton? No balls, just an innocent little birdie."

"I got through it in gym. But it seemed stupid to me. Why all the questions about my lack of sports prowess?"

He lifted one shoulder. "I don't know. I know Julia is into it. I'm surprised you're not."

"I'm Italian, Liam. Italian girls don't like to get sweaty or break nails. And Julia just likes to watch sports. Although I think she played softball in high school."

"She plays tennis, too. We played a few times last summer when she came to visit at my parents' house."

I dropped my eyes. It shouldn't have bothered me when Liam casually mentioned time spent with his ex-girlfriend. After all, I'd lived through their relationship, albeit from the other side. None of this was a surprise to me. I knew how things had ended, and I didn't have a speck of worry that Liam was still interested in Julia or vice verse. Over the last two weeks, they had settled into a sort of détente that was neither easy nor uncomfortable. Liam tended to come over to our room on the nights Julia was staying with Jesse, and if she were planning to stay at the dorm, he usually suggested that we meet at Beans or the student union.

But still ...it was a cold and hard fact that on the surface at least, Julia and Liam had more in common than he and I did. While Julia's family wasn't involved in politics and didn't have quite the same kind of money that the Baileys did, they were comfortable. I knew she only still lived with me in the dorms because I needed the RA gig to help with my room and board. She could have moved into an apartment off-campus, but she hadn't.

And why did this even matter to me? Liam and I had carefully stuck to our friendship pact since that morning at Jeff's house. He hadn't tried to touch me beyond a joking poke in the shoulder or elbow to the ribs. If on some level it hurt that he didn't even attempt anything more, that was clearly just an indication that I really was messed up.

"Hey. Earth to Ava. Did you hear me?"

I managed a smile. "Sorry. I zoned out for a minute. What did you say?"

Liam's mouth turned down, and his forehead drew together. "I asked if you wanted to come to my track meet Thursday."

I bit my lip. "I don't know, Liam. Do you think that's a good idea?"

"Why wouldn't it be? I don't remember any mention of not attending each other's sporting events in the rules."

"Because ...because Julia used to go to all your meets. And some people might think it's strange if I showed up now."

Liam gripped the back of the wooden chair, leaning to the side. "Julia used to come, yes. When she was my girlfriend. You being there won't be strange to anyone. Giff's probably going to come, too, if that makes you feel any better. And I don't care what some people might think. They can go fuck themselves."

I raised my eyebrows. "Well, that was oddly aggressive."

He ran a hand through his hair, leaving it standing on end. "Sorry. My mom and dad have been on this 'what will people say' kick again. It just pisses me off. I mean, who cares? Everyone believes what they're going to believe, right? I can't control that."

I nodded slowly. Liam's relationship with his parents was complicated, I knew, and lately any mention of them seemed to make him tense.

"What time on Thursday?"

"Hmmm?" He looked down at me, confused.

"The track meet. What time is it?"

"Oh. Ah, four o'clock."

"Okay. I'll be there."

"Really?" His face lit up, and a thrill clutched my chest that it mattered that much to him. That *I* mattered that much.

"Sure. I mean, sweaty guys in shorts running, jumping, throwing heavy stuff? What's not to like? I can't promise I won't ogle, but I'll try not to embarrass you."

He lifted his eyebrows. "You're going to check out other guys?"

I grinned. "Is that a problem, friend?"

Liam sighed and rubbed his face. "You're going to kill me, you know that, right?"

"What do you mean?" I cocked my head.

"Nothing. I gotta go. I'll talk to you tomorrow."

SPENDING A SPRING afternoon at a college track meet was not the worst use of my time, I decided as I climbed up the bleachers alongside the track. The sun was warm, the breeze kept it pleasant, and the place was swarming with tall young men in various states of undress. I watched one of them strip off his t-shirt, his muscles tensing and stretching with the effort beneath his tanned skin.

Yeah, not bad at all.

I scanned the area for Liam, but I didn't see him right away. The visiting team, dressed in black and gold, warmed up in the middle of the field, and the guys from Birch were trickling out of the locker room slowly but surely.

"Hey, peaches, enjoying the show?"

I grinned at Giff as he dropped down next to me. "You know it. I'm beginning to think I've been missing something all this time. Who knew all this hot testosterone was coming together right here on campus? It should be part of orientation."

"Yeah, they could save all the school spirit crap and just show footage from the meets. Girls would be here in droves. And some guys." He bumped his shoulder against mine.

"Speaking of which, is Jeff coming?"

"Nah. He's working until seven." Jeff had a job off-campus, working at the hardware store his uncle owned. Between those hours, his school work and his spot on the wrestling team, he was a busy guy.

"So it's just you and me. Cool. I don't have to pretend to be all feminist-savvy and act like I don't care about all the skin showing out there."

"Never around me, sweetie. I might be taken, but looking's free."

The coach of the visiting school gathered his team around him. Birch seemed to still be straggling onto the track, though some of them were stretching already.

I knew the minute Liam came out. We were too far away for me to see his face, but I recognized him by the way he moved, that stride that was both relaxed and aware. The white team shirt he wore was just tight enough that I could see the broad expanse of his chest, and the sleeves gave me a tantalizing view of his toned arms. His legs below the burgundy shorts were long and knotted with muscles, covered with a dusting of fine brown hair that I couldn't see from here.

My eyes followed him as he joined the rest of his team, standing with his hands on his hips and listening to the coach. When the older man clapped once, they all dispersed around the center of the track, warming up in small groups. Liam joined two other guys at the edge of the grass and began stretching, extending and flexing his legs.

He turned so that he faced us for the first time, and my heart sped up a little as I felt his eyes searching the bleachers. I could tell when he spotted me by the way he froze for just a few seconds. My mouth went dry, and I would have sworn I could actually feel him touching me, a line of heat spreading from my center up over my body. When he turned around again, I leaned back against my elbows and released a breath I hadn't realized I'd been holding.

Next to me, Giff shook his head. "You two ..." He sighed. "One of these days, I'm going to sit you both down and knock your heads together until you see sense. Or maybe lock you in a room. Jeff says I need to let you find your own way, but I'm losing patience."

My face still burned. "I don't know what you're talking about."

"And that's exactly what I mean. You walk into the room, and his eyes never leave you. When you don't think he's paying attention, you look at him like he's the last truffle in the box. You're both so damned stubborn."

"Giff, it's not that simple. We're friends. Let's be happy about that. The last few weeks have been the most fun I've had in a long time, because we just hang out, talk, study ...it's the best I can do."

He snorted. "Sure it is. I just hope you don't let it go too long. I've never seen Liam act like this about any girl. I thought Jules was pretty special, but you know, he was just going through the motions most of the time. When he talks about you, there's a tone in his voice ..." He glanced over at me and shook his head. "Forget it. Minding my own business now. Look, the first event is starting."

Liam ran the 800 and the 1500 meter races, and then he was part of the relay. I stood up with everyone else, screaming for him, clapping madly when they won. I watched him bend over at waist, his shoulders heaving with the effort of catching his breath. He raised his head and looked straight at me, eyes hot, mouth parted as he panted. With every fiber of my being, I wanted to cross the track, take his sweaty head between my hands and cover his open mouth with mine. Thrust my tongue between his lips until he lowered me to the grass ...

"Ava? You okay, peaches?" Giff slung an arm around my shoulder. "You look like you're about to pass out. Here, sit down."

As I sank back onto the cold metal bench, I heard the two girls behind me sighing. "Oh my God. Liam Bailey can do me any time. He's the hottest one out there, and it has nothing to do with running."

"Yeah, I bet he's got endurance ..." They both giggled.

I closed my eyes. Listening to them reminded me that I'd be crazy to think about Liam as anything but a friend. He was miles out of my league. Plus, there was the little fact that I wasn't looking for entanglement, even if the reasons why were unclear just now.

The meet ended, and Giff grabbed my arm. "Come on. I'm going to say hi to Liam before he goes to the locker room."

He stood at the chain link fence, leaning his arms against the rail as he watched us approach. I hung back a little, letting Giff take the lead.

"Nice job, bro." Giff fist-bumped him, and Liam grinned.

"Thanks for coming. Not bad today. What are you doing now?"

"Heading over to Jeff's. I'm going to try to make dinner for when he gets home from work. Jules gave me a recipe for mac and cheese that she swears I can't screw up. I guess we'll see."

"Cool. See you tomorrow."

"Yeah, see you." Giff glanced back at me. "Bye, peaches. Remember what we talked about."

I nodded, moistening my lips nervously as Giff loped

away. When I finally looked back at Liam, he was staring at my mouth. The unguarded want in his eyes shot straight to my core, and I couldn't breathe. I reached for the cool silver bar at the top of the fence and held on with both hands, just to keep from sinking to the ground in a puddle of need.

"I'm glad you came." His words, low and husky, didn't help me at all.

"So am I," I managed to say. "You looked good. I mean, the runs. The races. The meet."

Liam straightened and slid his hands so that they covered mine on the fence. His skin was hot on the backs of my fingers, and I wanted to moan when he rubbed his palms lightly over my knuckles.

"Do you have any plans? For the rest of the day, I mean. For tonight." His voice sounded strained, and I glanced into his face. His jaw was clenched as though he were holding himself in tight control.

"Um ...nothing. No plans."

"Want to go have dinner with me? I just have to grab a shower and change."

I nodded. "Okay. Sure. I can do that. Do you want to meet me some place?"

"No, I'll pick you up at your room in half an hour, all right?"

"Yeah." I didn't move. The weight of his hands, still holding mine, kept me in place.

"Hey, Ava?"

"Yeah?" I repeated.

"Wear that skirt, okay? The black one from Jeff's party?"

I swallowed hard, sure I was about to spontaneously combust. I wanted to make some flip remark about how friends didn't make wardrobe demands like that, but I couldn't do it. Instead I just nodded again.

"I will."

Ch♥pter Ten

LIAM KNOCKED AT my door about twenty minutes after I'd left him at the track. I was just slipping on shoes.

"You're early," I greeted him.

He shrugged. "Motivated." He swept his gaze down my body, and his lips curled in appreciation. "God, you look good."

I gave him a teasing smile. "What, this old thing? Someone I know told me to wear it."

I'd paired the same tank and skirt as I had at Jeff's party, but since we were going to a restaurant tonight instead of a barbecue, tonight I wore strappy black heels. I had to admit, my legs, which I always thought were stumpy and short, looked good.

Liam had dressed up, too. The khakis were pressed, and the blue polo matched his eyes. His hair was still damp from the shower, and before I could stop myself, I reached up to flip one light brown curl out of his eyes.

The minute I touched his skin, Liam grabbed my arm in a grip of steel. "Don't," he breathed. "Ava, I'm trying.

I'm trying to stick to what you want. Friendship only. But right now, it's hard to remember why."

I couldn't speak. My tongue was paralyzed as he slid his hand down my arm and then held me by the shoulders.

"At this minute, all I can think is that I want to back you into the wall, lift up that skirt and drive into you. Wrap your gorgeous legs around my waist, with your heels still on, so I can feel them against my back. Fill my hands with your tits, suck your nipples into my mouth. Pound myself inside you until you come so loud and hard, you scream my name loud enough for the whole building to hear."

My pulse was beating so fast that I felt it throughout my body. I knew if I made one move, I'd pull Liam's mouth down to mine and then everything would happen just as he had just said.

And that was a problem why? I couldn't quite remember.

I opened my mouth, but before I could speak, Liam dropped his hands from my arms. "Come on. Let's go while I can still walk." He turned his back to me, fists clenched at his sides.

I picked up my purse and slung it over my shoulder, locked the door and closed it behind me. Liam didn't turn around. He began walking as soon as the door clicked shut.

The drive to the restaurant was quiet. I was afraid to say anything, but after a few minutes, Liam began talking about the meet, the other school's track team and some of his own teammates. I asked him questions about a few of the events and why he stuck to the middle distance runs.

"I used to be a sprinter, but I found out I like the races that are a little longer better. I might start doing some long-distance races, too. I run cross country in the fall, and that helps."

He pulled up in front of a small restaurant on the main street of the next town over. I smiled as I saw the sign.

"Italian, huh? You're a brave man."

He shrugged. "I figured it was a safe bet that you'd like it." He met me on my side of the car, opening the door before I could, and took my hand to help me out. At his touch, I felt a tremor shoot up my arm.

Liam shut the car door, and then he moved the hand holding mine behind his back. I had no choice but to snug my body against his, with my arm wrapped around his waist. His other hand came up to caress the side of my face.

"Just one kiss. Out here, in the open, where it's safe that I won't get carried away."

He tilted his head so that our foreheads touched and looked deep into my eyes. I realized he was waiting for my decision.

I had no choice. No matter what logic or reason might say, I had only one answer. I nodded, the slightest movement of my head.

Liam didn't hesitate. He angled his mouth over mine, soft and teasing until I sagged in his hold. Then he brushed his tongue over my lips, insistent, and I opened them with a soft noise in the back of my throat. He swept over my teeth, circled my tongue and traced lines on the sides of my mouth.

He released me with one small kiss to the side of my lips, and then leaned to my ear so that I heard his words like a whisper.

"God, I want you, Ava."

I stumbled when Liam stepped back, but he held tight to my hand. I followed him into the restaurant.

The sights and smells were so familiar that it was like coming home. I was still shaken by Liam's kiss, but being in this restaurant settled me. We followed the hostess to a small round table near the windows.

"Seriously, is this okay? I've been here with my parents a few times, and their food's decent."

"Yeah, of course it is." I glanced around the dim room, lit only with candles on the table tops. "It reminds me so much of my family's place. And that's a very good thing."

Liam raised his brows. "Your family's place? You have a restaurant?"

I grinned. "Didn't you know that? My grandparents opened it in the fifties. Now my parents run it. Well, all of us pitch in. I started out as a busgirl when I was ten and got promoted to waitress when I was sixteen."

Liam sat back in his chair. "How did I not know this about you? It's not like you never talk about your family."

"I don't make a big deal about it. It's just what we do. But most people at Birch eat at big city restaurants—a little family place down by the shore wouldn't mean anything to them."

"Are you close to your parents?" Liam picked up his menu and scanned it, but I had a feeling he wasn't really seeing it.

I thought for a minute. "I am. We've always been a tight family, I think. I mean, we're Italian. We're loud, and we don't let things fester. But then a few years back, we had something happen, and it made us even more aware of ..." I tried to think of the best way to say it without sounding trite. "I guess, how important family is. How things can change in the blink of an eye. So we try to appreciate each other more. We don't waste time. Do you know what I mean?"

Liam stared at me over the top of the laminated sheet in his hand, his brow furrowed. "I think so. Not that I've had that happen, but I know what you're talking about."

His eyes flickered down. "Can I ask what happened that changed everything?"

I licked my lip. I didn't talk about Antonia; only a select few people at Birch knew what had happened, but it wasn't a secret.

"My sister Antonia was killed by a drunk driver."

"God, Ava, I'm sorry." Liam reached across to squeeze my hand. "That's awful. Was she older than you?"

"Yes, by two years."

"Were you close?"

I smiled. "Oh, yeah. We used to get into trouble together, and we loved the same music, and the same movies ..." Sudden, unexpected tears filled my eyes. "I wish you had known her. She was ...wonderful."

"I wish I had, too." Liam stared at me intently, a small line between his eyes. "I always wanted a sister or brother. I thought it might take some of the pressure off me."

"I can't imagine life without my brothers. Hard enough missing Antonia. I'm sorry you never had that."

The waitress stepped up to the table and took our drink and appetizer order. Liam ordered us a bottle of wine, shooting me a grin.

"Wine okay? I know you'd probably rather have jungle juice, but I'm pretty sure they won't serve that here."

I made a face at him. "Ugh. Don't bring that up, or I might not be able to eat my dinner."

Our meal was simple, filling food, and I was surprised at how relaxed I was. Liam made me laugh by telling me stories of his growing up.

"My parents insisted that they take me to these stupid political events so I'd get a taste for it, but God, it was boring. I used to make up terrible stuff to do, just to liven it up for me. Or maybe it was that I was trying to be a brat, so they wouldn't make me go anymore."

"What's the worst thing you ever did?" I bit into my crusty bread.

"Hmmm ..." Liam rolled his eyes back, thinking. "Well, there was this one fund raising dinner. I must have been about eight. It felt like the speeches were never going to end. As long as I was quiet, no one really paid any attention to me. I drank so much water, just sitting there, that I had to go to the bathroom, like every ten minutes. I'd just get up and go into the men's room, nobody noticed. Then I decided to make it more fun. I took a handful of silverware off the table every time I went to the restroom and hid it in the plant in there. It was like a game, to see how much I could take from the table before someone caught me. They never did, but by the time the speeches were over and they served dessert, there wasn't a single piece left on the table."

I laughed. "You were evil! Oh my God, Liam, I can just see you, this adorable little boy, creeping around to steal knives."

He leaned forward. "How do you know I was adorable?"

I shrugged. "I can't see you being anything but."

Liam held my eyes for a minute. I thought he was going to say something, but he seemed to change his mind. The spell was broken when the waitress brought us a plate of tiramisu for dessert. I took one bite and then sat back, holding my stomach.

"I can't eat anything else, or I'm going to explode. This was so good, Liam. Thanks."

He smiled as he forked another piece into his mouth. "Hey, Amanda texted me today. She invited us all to a party on Saturday night for her boyfriend's birthday. It's at a dance club in the city. Want to go?"

I shook my head. "I wish I could. But I have to go

home this weekend."

"Home? To your parents' house?"

I nodded. "Yeah. My brother's getting married in three weeks. I'm in the wedding, and I've got to get one more fitting on my dress. My mom's been bugging me about it, and I keep putting it off, but she put her foot down—it's got to be this week."

Liam laid the fork down on the plate. "Okay. Can I go with you?"

I couldn't have been more shocked if he had suggested we fly to Mars for the weekend. "Come with me? Home? Why?"

He cocked his head. "I don't know. Meet your parents? So you don't have to make the drive by yourself? To eat at your family's restaurant? Why not?"

I took a deep breath. "Liam, I'm not sure you understand what you're saying. I—if I bring you home, my parents are going to make some big assumptions, no matter how much I tell them we're just friends. I've never brought anyone home with me. Well, except Julia, of course."

"And she lived to tell the tale. I feel pretty safe. Come on, why not? If I don't go with you, I'll just sit around my room, being bored all weekend. You don't want that on your conscience, do you?"

"I thought you were invited to Amanda's party," I reminded him.

"I don't want to go without you."

"Liam, friendship, remember? You go places without Giff. You don't need me."

He snagged my hand again and laced his fingers through mine. "If you think that's true, you're blind." His thumb tucked between our hands and traced circles against my palm, making me shiver.

"I'm pretty sure this is against the rules." But I didn't even try to pull my hand away.

"Fuck the rules." He almost whispered the words, with a half-smile on his face taking away the force of what he said. "I've tried, Ava. I think I did pretty damn good being your friend. Hands off, no commitment, no pressure. But I want more, and I think you do, too. Even if you won't admit it."

I blew out a sigh. I couldn't argue with him, not when the touch of his thumb made me want to slither onto the floor.

"I promise, no pushing. Let me come home with you this weekend. I'll do my best to stick to the friendship deal. I can't say I won't try to kiss you when we're alone, but I'll respect whatever you want to tell your parents about us. Okay?"

I was sure that tonight, alone in the rational darkness, without Liam holding my hand, I'd come up with a hundred reasons to say no. But sitting here, I couldn't think of one.

"Okay."

"YOU'RE GOING *WHERE* with *who*?"

Julia stared at me as though I'd grown a second head. I'd waited to tell her about my weekend plans on purpose, on a hunch she might have this response. Turns out I wasn't wrong.

"I'm going home to get fitted for my bridesmaid dress. My mom and Angela are having fits because I haven't done it yet. Carl texted me on Monday, begging me to just get it done before they drive him crazy."

"That part I get. But why is Liam going with you?"

I kept my smile even. "Just to keep me company on the drive. You know. As a friend."

"Bullshit." Julia shook her head. "Ava, are you crazy?"

"No. And don't make it a big deal. It isn't."

"What are your parents going to think?"

I swallowed. I hadn't quite decided how to deal with that part of the weekend yet. "They'll be fine. They didn't have a problem when I brought you home with me."

Julia snorted. "I wasn't trying to get into your pants."

"Well, that's a disappointment. Here I'd been hoping this whole Jesse thing was just a phase, and you'd come back to my loving arms."

"Ava, I'm serious. You're playing with fire. Liam ...he's messing with you. You're going to end up getting hurt."

Irritation flared. "Why? Because I'm too stupid, too naïve to know better?"

Julia flushed. "No. Of course not. Ava, you're the most intelligent person I know. But I think maybe you have a blind spot when it comes to Liam."

"You think you know him better than I do?" It was a sore point with me, I realized, that Julia had been privy to so much more of Liam's life. Maybe she did know him better. In at least one way she did. I bit my lip and tried to drive that thought from my mind.

As though she could read my mind, Julia looked sick. "No. I don't think I know him better, because I don't think Liam lets anyone in to know him. I dated him for ten months. I met his parents, I knew his friends, and yes, let's not dance around this, I slept with him. But I still don't think I really knew him."

It was on the tip of my tongue to tell her it was different with Liam and me. But she was never going to be-lieve something I wasn't even sure was true. So instead I retreated to my default position.

"We're just friends, Jules. I don't have any delusions about Liam. Please try not to worry."

She shook her head. "I can't promise anything. But Ava, please be careful."

After that conversation, I was even more reluctant about the phone call I knew I had to make. I waited until Saturday morning, when I knew my mother would be on her way into the restaurant.

"Ava, what's the matter?"

I smiled. My mom answered every one of my phone calls that way, unless it was our planned bi-weekly chat.

"Nothing's wrong, Ma. Why would something be wrong?"

"You're going to be here in a few hours, and you're telephoning me. So I figure something must be up. Are you on the road? Are you using your headset? You know it's illegal to talk in the car without your hands-free."

"No, I'm not on the road yet. I'm leaving in about an hour. But Ma, I wanted to tell you something real fast be-fore I leave. I'm bringing a friend with me, if that's okay."

"Why wouldn't it be okay? Of course. Are you bring-ing Julia?"

"No, not Jules. His name is Liam. Liam Bailey."

The silence on the other end of the line was fright-ening. I could picture my mother, standing in the kitchen, getting ready for the day at the restaurant, her handbag on the chair by the door, sunglasses on her head. Holding the phone against her shoulder, because God for-bid she only do one thing at once. And right now, the look on her face was likely a mix of shock and joy. With a healthy dose of apprehension, too.

"A boy? You're bringing home a boy?"

"Ma, calm down. He's just a friend. Got that? Just. A. Friend."

"But he's a boy."

"He is. But Ma, promise you won't embarrass me. And tell the boys, too. No teasing, no making a fuss. Got it?"

"Embarrass you? Ava Catarine, when has your family ever embarrassed you?"

"Don't make me give you a list, Ma. You'll be late for opening up."

My mother said something low under her breath that I'm fairly sure was a curse. As loud and over the top as my family could be, my mother was always a lady, and she never resorted to what she called vulgarities except under the most trying circumstances.

"Fine, all right. We won't make a fuss. Well, I won't, and I'll warn the boys, but I can't speak for your father."

I laughed. "Daddy's the least of my worries."

"Oh, sure, sweetie, you just wait. Cripes, I gotta go. Listen, this boy, will he need his own bedroom?"

"Oh my God, Ma, what are you saying? What if I said, no, he's sleeping in with me? What would you do?"

"I'm just asking. I don't know what goes on at college, I want to ask the question so I can have a bed ready for him. How about I put him in your room, and you can sleep in with Frankie?"

"That's fine. Whatever's easiest. Listen, Ma, you need to go, and so do I. I'll see you tonight. We'll come by the restaurant for dinner, okay? Save me some gnocchi. And some of the good bread."

I hung up up and fell back onto my bed, utterly exhausted. Maybe Julia was right. This weekend was going to be a disaster.

Ch♥pter Eleven

"SO TELL ME about your family."

Liam's BMW flew along the two-lane back roads, as the pine barrens passed in a blur. I leaned back in the leather seat and watched him out of the corner of my eye.

"What do you want to know?"

"Everything. How many brothers do you have?"

"Two, and they're both older than me. Carl—his real name is Carlo, and he's the one getting married, to Angela. He's twenty-six. And Vince, he's twenty-five. He was dating a girl, but they broke up last winter."

"Do they both work at the restaurant?"

"Yeah. Carl is more in the business end. He handles the suppliers, promotion, all the legal stuff. And Vince went to pastry school, so he does the desserts. But they both cook, too, if we're short."

"Who cooks usually?"

"My mom, sometimes my dad, and my aunt Lorena. She's my dad's sister. And if my grandparents are up from Florida, they pitch in, too. It can get pretty crazy."

"I can't imagine." There was a trace of envy in Liam's voice. "In my family ...that would never happen."

"Tell me about them."

He glanced at me. "Who? My parents?"

"Yeah. You're going to meet mine in a few hours. The crazy will be right there for you to see. The least you can do is give me some dirt on your family. It'll make me feel better."

He didn't smile. "My parents ...are very private, very ..." He was searching for the word, I could tell. "Very controlled people. My dad thinks everything can be manipulated. He's never come across a situation he couldn't fix with money or influence. He doesn't get that sometimes people can't be fixed that way."

There was anger beneath his words, and I reached out my hand to take his. "I'm sorry. But they love you. It might be in a different way than what I'm used to, but they do."

"Maybe." He tightened his hold on my hand, and his lips pressed together.

I stared out the window for a few minutes, trying to think of some way to change the subject, something to lighten his mood. What popped into my mind might not have been the smartest bet, but the words were tumbling out of my mouth before I could stop and think.

"Julia thought I was crazy to let you come home with me this weekend." I tilted my head, studying his profile. "She says I don't know you."

Liam jerked his eyes toward me, frowning. "And she thinks she does?"

"No, that was kind of her point. That even after dating you for that long, she doesn't feel like she knows the real you."

"She's probably right." He sounded thoughtful. "It's

not like we spent long hours talking. Okay, so what do you want to know about me?"

I laughed. "That's not how it works. You get to know people by spending time with them, having real conversations, listening to each other."

"In which case, you know me better than Julia. She and I didn't have many conversations that didn't end in us fighting."

"That's true. Well, what do you know about me?"

He smiled, one of his rare sweet genuine smiles. "I know you're very focused on your future, and you're ambitious. I know you're compassionate and kind, even when people make you impatient. I know your favorite color is blue, and you love Frank Sinatra."

I cocked one eyebrow in surprise. "How do you know that? About Frank?"

"I looked at your 'most played songs' play list on your phone. Lots of Ol' Blue Eyes."

I lifted my shoulder. "I know it's not cool, but what can I say? He's Italian, he's a Jersey boy, and his music ..." I sighed. "It makes me swoon."

"I was hoping that was the case." He leaned forward and pushed a button on the sound system. Immediately the car was flooded with music as Frank sang about flying to the moon.

I squealed my seldom-heard fan-girl cry. "How did you do that?"

"Made a play list of Sinatra and downloaded it to my system here. It's under 'Ava'."

"Liam." Tears sprang to my eyes. "I don't know what to say. This is wonderful."

His hand gripped mine a little tighter. "I'm glad you like it. You know, it's rumored that Frank's one great love was Ava Gardner. She kept him waiting, too. Made him work for her."

"Is that what I'm doing? Making you work for me?" His voice was barely above a whisper. "I hope so."

I closed my eyes, listening to the music, and sighed. "So this proves you know me. But I'm not sure it works the other way. If someone asked me to make a play list for you, I'm not sure I could."

Liam nodded. "Want to know a secret? I'm not sure you'll believe me, but Frank would be on my list, too. My mom's father ...he passed away when I was sixteen. But I used to go spend summers with him, and he played Sinatra all the time. All the big band music, really. And we would watch the old movies, too. Have you ever seen *High Society*, with Frank and Bing Crosby and Grace Kelly?"

"And Satchmo!" I grinned. "I used to watch those with my dad. So we've got Sinatra in common. A love for old movies and big band music. And I think your favorite color is ..." I cast my eyes up, thinking. "Green."

"You're right. How did you know?"

"It was a total guess. Guys are hard to figure out, but the comforter on your bed is green, so I went with it."

"Okay. See? You know me pretty well."

"Uh-huh. So what's going on with your parents?"

He sucked in a quick breath. "What are you talking about?"

"Every time you mention your mom and dad, you get a look on your face. And they haven't been down to see you lately, even though I remember when you were dating Jules, they were here a lot. So what's going on?"

"It's ...complicated."

I shook my head. "That's the word you use every tine you don't want to talk about something. If you want to tell me it's none of my business, that's fine."

He sighed. "No. I'm just not sure myself about who

my mom and dad are anymore. It's hard to explain to someone else. I always thought I knew my parents pretty well. I didn't like what they did or said all the time, but I never thought ...that there were things they were hiding. And now it feels like everything is a lie, everything they told me and taught me. I can't trust them."

"I'm sorry." I released his hand to run my fingers up his forearm. "I can't imagine how hard that must be. My mom and dad make me crazy, but we're not the type of people to have any secrets."

"I didn't think we were, either. I was wrong." He paused. "And then there's the whole politics thing. When you asked me that night why I was going into something I didn't want, it opened my mind. I want to do something else. But they won't hear it. Or me."

"Maybe if you have a good plan about what you want to do, they'll understand." I felt the muscles in his arm tense beneath my touch. "I'm always around if you need someone to talk to about it."

"Thanks." He took a deep breath. "Ava, I never want to tell you not to touch me, because, God, when you do ...but if you keep doing what you're doing right now, I'm going to have to pull over. And I'm not sure we'll make it to your parents' house."

I froze, my hand in mid-stroke. And then I moved it back to my own lap, carefully. "Sorry."

He looked over at me ruefully. "Never apologize. Not for that."

THE ARRIVAL AT my house was anticlimactic, because everyone was at the restaurant. I unlocked the front door and led Liam inside.

I had never been to his house, of course, but I'd seen Julia's pictures, and I could imagine. So I found myself trying to excuse the cozy house where I'd been raised.

"Ava." Liam laid a hand on my shoulder. "Stop. The house is great." He lifted our two bags. "Where do you want me to take these?"

"Follow me." I led him up the narrow staircase to the second floor, where three bedrooms and a bath crowded around the hall. "You'll be here in my room." I pointed to the closed door, and Liam looked at me with a surprised smile and raised eyebrows.

"Frank really did the trick, didn't he?"

I rolled my eyes. "No, you goof. You're sleeping in my room, but I'm not. I'm going to sleep with Frankie." I leaned around him and opened my bedroom door.

Liam glanced around the room that had been mine from birth until I left for college. A few photos were still hanging up, along with the academic awards and ribbons I'd earned.

"Nice." He set down his bag. "Now who the hell is Frankie?"

"Hmm?" I looked up at him, frowning.

"You said you're sleeping with Frankie. You told me your brothers are Carl and Vince. So unless your dog Frankie has his own room ...I need an explanation. If I can't sleep with you, why can Frankie?"

I shook my head. "Sorry. I forgot I hadn't told you ...Frankie is my niece. She's Antonia's daughter."

"I thought Antonia ..." He didn't finish the thought.

"Yes, you're right. Um, it's complicated, as you would say."

When he tilted his head, I sighed. "Antonia got pregnant when she was a junior in high school. It was ...a big

147

deal in my family. I know for most people, having a baby without being married isn't the end of the world now, but for us, it was. My parents were devastated. Antonia was smart. Like, much more so than me. She probably could have gone to any college she wanted, on a full scholarship. But she was fun, too—she could hang out with her friends, go to parties and still get a hundred on a test the next day."

"What about the baby's father?"

I made a face. "He was guy she had been dating for a long time. But when she got pregnant, he dumped her. I guess his parents offered to help out with some of the costs, but my parents refused. They made him relinquish his paternal rights after Antonia died, so they have full custody of Frankie."

Liam rubbed my back. "I'm sorry, I didn't mean to pry."

"No, I meant to say something. You'll meet her tonight at the restaurant."

I took my bag and tossed it into Frankie's tiny room, and then offered Liam my hand.

"Are you ready to face the music? Time to meet my family."

SATURDAY NIGHT AT Cucina Felice meant a parking lot overflowing with cars and lines out the door. I felt a sense of satisfaction and pride as we pulled in.

"Drive around back. There's a family section fenced off for us to park." When Liam pulled up to the gate, I jumped out to type in the code that hadn't changed since I was a child.

We locked the car, and I made my way back out, slipping between the edge of the fence and the hedge. Liam held my hand, his fingers rubbing against the back of my knuckles in such a way that I knew he was nervous.

"What does the name mean? Cucina Felice ...it's kitchen something, right?"

I nodded. "Happy Kitchen. My grandmother always says a happy kitchen is the heart of the family, and she had so much family, she had to open a restaurant to have a big enough heart."

I could have taken him in the back door, but I had enough pride in what my family had accomplished to want to show off a little. We crossed the green lawn and climbed the steps to the porch. A few people called my name in greeting, and I waved.

"Friends of yours?" Liam leaned to whisper in my ear.

I smiled. "Small town. Everyone knows everyone."

Angela, who was shortly to be my new sister-in-law, was working the hostess stand. She was talking to a tiny white-haired lady as we came up.

"Yes, Mrs. Collini, the cake is all set. We'll bring it out right after the coffee is served."

"All right, but not before. I want it to surprise Mr. Collini, but I don't want the cake sitting on the table while we wait for coffee."

Angela smiled. "No, ma'am. I've reminded your server. You can just relax and enjoy your special evening."

Mollified, the lady tottered back to her table, and Angela turned to us, still wearing her professional smile, which widened to a grin.

"Ava! Oh, thank God you're here. I was so worried about your dress, all the other girls have theirs done and already back at home with them, and I was thinking ..."

She glanced behind me and got an eyeful of Liam. Her mouth fell open.

"Ange, this is my friend Liam. Liam, this is Angela—"

The rest of my words were lost in her shriek. "Oh my God, Ava, you brought home a boy!"

Every head in the restaurant turned to us. There were mostly smiles, along with a few smirks and snickers, from people who had known me most of my life.

Liam handled the whole thing like a pro. He returned Angela's hug and nodded to whatever questions she was shooting at him. I tried to pull him away, but she wouldn't let go.

Across the restaurant, standing right outside the kitchen, I spotted my mother. She was standing against the wall, watching the whole debacle with a smile on her face. I recognized that smile. It was the same expression she wore when she'd been proved right in some argument with me. And it all clicked.

"Angela, we'll talk to you later. We need to go say hello to Ma and the boys. And is Daddy here, too?"

"Yeah, he's in the kitchen tonight. Everyone's in the kitchen, we're slammed."

I patted her arm and dragged Liam into the dining room, trying to ignore the knowing smiles from the patrons.

"I'm sorry about that." I had to almost shout to be heard.

"Why? She's great." Liam spoke into my ear.

I shook my head as we reached Ma. She hadn't moved.

"Okay, Ma, well-played."

My mother raised her eyebrows and cocked her head. "What on earth do you mean, Ava?"

"Angela! I know you heard her, because I'm pretty sure everyone in the tri-state area heard her. You didn't tell her not to make a fuss."

She smiled again. "You didn't mention Angela. You said I shouldn't make a fuss, and I should tell the boys, too. I did. You never mentioned Angela."

And this was why my mother would always be my hero.

"Ma, this is my *friend* Liam. Liam, this is my mother, Francesca DiMartino."

Liam offered his hand. "Mrs. DiMartino, thank you for your hospitality. You have a lovely home, and your restaurant—"

Before he could finish, Ma had disregarded his hand and pulled him into a hug. "Liam, welcome! So glad you're here. Come, we've got a little table for you and Ava Catarine. We'll bring food."

She hauled him over to a corner table for two, while I trailed in their wake. Liam sat down, as my mother shook out the linen napkin and laid it on his lap. I dropped into the other chair and got my own napkin.

"Now, tonight our special is the cioppino. You like seafood, don't you?"

Liam nodded.

"Excellent. We'll start with a salad and then gnocchi with marinara, because no one leaves Cucina Felice without sampling my husband's marinara. I'll send one of the girls over with some bread and olive oil."

"Hey, Ma? Remember me, your daughter?"

My mother spared me a look. "Ava, behave. You have a guest. We want him to feel welcome."

"Fine. Oh, and I'm glad you're not fussing, by the way. Is Frankie here?"

Ma nodded. "Of course. She's back in the kitchen,

coloring. I'll send her out."

When my mother finally left us alone, I leaned forward to apologize again to Liam. A tall shadow fell across the table.

"Ava, thank God you came home. Angela and Ma were making me crazy over that dress." Carl set a basket of bread on the table. He spoke to me, but I noticed his eyes kept darting to Liam.

"I'm sorry it took me so long. School's been really busy. Carl, this is my friend Liam. Liam, my brother Carl."

Carl held it together admirably, shaking Liam's hand as though I brought a guy home every weekend. I was pretty sure I was the only one who noticed my brother's lips twitching as he surreptitiously checked him out.

"Okay, I gotta get back in the kitchen before Ma pitches a tizzy. Enjoy." He gave us a nod before he turned.

"I like him." Liam smiled as he broke off a piece of bread and dipped it in the olive oil.

"Yeah, he's terrific. I'm sorry about how crazy—"

"Auntie Ave!"

I was hit on the side by a miniature tornado of energy. Laughing, I reached down to scoop her up.

"Francesca! You've grown a foot! Are you driving yet?"

She giggled, scrambling onto my lap. "No, I can't drive, I'm only little. But Nonna let me roll the gnocchi tonight and she said I did it even better than you."

I grimaced. "Sorry to burst your bubble, kid, but that doesn't take much."

She laughed again, snuggling against my chest in a way that always gave me a pang. She was a child who was so loved, so treasured, and yet she didn't remember her own mother. I rubbed my cheek against her silky black hair. When I glanced up, Liam was watching me, an odd look on his face.

"Frankie, I want you to meet my friend Liam. He came up from college with me. Liam, this little terror is Frankie."

He leaned over to grin into her face. "Nice to meet you, Miss Frankie."

She blushed and rolled her eyes up to me. I sighed. Liam's effect on females obviously knew no age boundaries.

"Frankie, you need to go back to the kitchen. Nonna says."

My brother Vince was carrying a tray of salads. He set two on our table, and I performed the introductions yet again. Vince didn't say much; he nodded, shook hands and then walked away.

"Is that everyone?" Liam asked, as he stabbed lettuce from his salad.

"Just Daddy. But you don't have to worry about him. He's very chill."

The food kept coming, and by the time the cioppino was set in front of us, Liam shook his head.

"I don't know if I can eat another bite." He had to yell to be heard, as the noise level had continued to amp up.

"What, no dessert?" I teased. "You're going to break my mother's heart."

Liam shook his head, his eyes never leaving mine. "The only dessert I could manage isn't on the menu. And I'm pretty sure it's not something I can enjoy in front of your family."

My face grew warm. "You're right about that." I picked up our plates. "We'll take it home and have it later. Wait here, and I'll get this wrapped. Then we can go back to the house. They probably need this table, anyway."

I carried the plates into the kitchen as quietly as I

could, hoping to get past my mother without being seen. No such luck.

"Ava, did he not like his food?" She crossed her arms over her chest as she stared me down. "And Vince made a rum cake. I was just about to cut you some and bring it out."

"No, Ma, it was wonderful, but you sent out so much, we were full before the main course came. I'm going to wrap it up and we'll take it home. Can you box up the cake, too?"

"Are you leaving?" The rise in her voice told me this might be a problem.

"Yeah, Ma. It's crowded here, and I'm tired. I just want to go be in the quiet."

"So you're taking that boy to the house while no one else is there?"

I bit back a smile. He had gone from being The Boy Ava Brought Home to That Boy. Feelings ran like quicksilver in my family.

"I'm going to the house. Liam is coming with me. If it'll make you feel better, we can take Frankie home, too, and put her to bed. Just to help you out."

My mother pursed her lips and probably would have said a lot more if a gentle voice hadn't cut across both of us.

"Francesca, leave the girl alone. She's a smart one, she's got a good head."

"Daddy!" I hugged my father, inhaling his unique aroma of tomatoes, light cologne and the faintest tinge of the pipe my mother pretended he never smoked.

"I was just out in the dining room and met your friend. Seems like a nice boy. I know of his father."

I wasn't sure what to say. "Okay. I'm sorry we didn't see you before. It's been bedlam out there."

My father smiled and held out his hands in a what-can-you-do gesture. "Saturday night. So you go on home, get some rest. We'll all talk tomorrow morning at breakfast."

"Anthony, but she's going home to be alone in the house. With a boy."

"Frannie." Daddy turned and laid his hands on my mother's shoulders. "She's a grown-up. She lives away from home. What she's going to do, she's going to do." He turned back to me. "But it would help us and set your mother's mind at ease if you took Frankie. Thanks for offering."

I stood on tip-toe to kiss my father's cheek. "Thank you, Daddy. 'Night, Ma. See you tomorrow morning."

Ch♥pter Twelve

IT WAS THREE in the afternoon by the time Liam and I left my parents' house the next day. The car was filled with packaged food, including the leftover cioppino, several loaves of bread and a box of my mother's cookies.

I had gotten up early that morning to go to Mass with my mother, knowing she expected it even if she didn't say anything. After we got home, I helped her put together the family breakfast that had been our tradition for as long as I could remember. As soon as we finished eating, Ma and Angela whisked me off to the bridal store for my fitting.

Liam and I hadn't had much chance to talk. The night before, Frankie had chattered all the way back to my parents' house. I had hoped she would settle down and fall asleep once we got home, but she insisted that I lay down with her. And of course, I went to sleep before she did.

"Well?" I glanced at him as we pulled away from the house. "Are you sorry you came? You could have had a nice quiet weekend partying with Amanda and Giff at a dance club in the city."

He didn't answer for a moment, and my stomach

dropped. Maybe he was thinking exactly what I had just said. Maybe he was thinking that he didn't want to have anything to do with someone who came from a hotbed of insanity. That possibility hurt me more than I could imagine.

"Do you know how lucky you are?" He looked over at me at last. "Do you realize that everyone in that house came up to me at one point in the time I was there and told me how wonderful you are? How I'd be fortunate if you and I were more than friends?" He frowned. "I'm pretty sure your brother Vince also threatened me if I did anything to hurt you. I'm not sure. He's kind of low-key."

I swallowed over the lump in my throat. "Yeah. They're nuts, but they're mine, I guess."

"I think your mother hugged me more in the fifteen hours we were there than my mother has in my memory." There was pain in his voice, and I longed to be able to take it away.

"We tend to be demonstrative. And loud. But you always know where you stand with them. If someone's mad, they yell and scream, and then it's over."

"I never know where I stand with my father. I'm pretty sure my mother's proud of me. I know she loves me in her way. But it's so much harder with my dad." He gripped the steering wheel a little harder. "Thank you for letting me come with you. It was ...wonderful."

I nodded, not sure of what else to say.

"Oh, and by the way, Carl and Angela invited me to their wedding. Are you by any chance looking for a date?"

I DIDN'T SEE Liam for several days after we got back from my parents' house. I had a few quizzes to study for, and Liam had an away track meet. He texted me often, sometimes serious, sometimes teasing. I wasn't sure where we stood. He had kissed my cheek after he left me in my room on Sunday afternoon, but I was sure part of the reason for that was Julia sitting on her bed, starring daggers at both of us.

I was walking back to the dorm after my last class on Wednesday when someone grabbed my arm and pulled me off the brick pathway.

"Hey!" I started indignantly, and then I saw Liam's teasing face.

"Sorry, didn't mean to startle you. You just looked so serious and intent walking along here ... I felt like the Big Bad Wolf, stalking Little Red Riding Hood."

I looked up at him, a smile playing around my lips. "So what does the wolf do with poor Red once he captures her?"

A slow grin spread across his face. "Hmmm. So many things. But maybe he starts here."

He lowered his mouth to mine, possessive and warm as he fitted me to him. I twined my arms up to wrap around his neck and opened my mouth to deepen the kiss.

Liam straightened after a minute, sighing into my hair. "I missed you. Wish I could take you back to my room right now and show you what else the wolf would do, but I'm running late to track practice."

I made a face. "Yeah, and I've got an RA council meeting tonight."

"Hmmm." He swung back toward the path, taking my hand as we walked. "What are you doing tomorrow?"

"After class? Nothing that I know of. Why?"

"Come running with me."

My feelings must have been evident on my face, because Liam laughed. "Come on. I promise, it'll be fun. I'll take it slow with you." He waggled his eyebrows, giving the words extra meaning.

"Liam, I don't run."

"How do you know? Have you ever tried?"

"No ...well, not really. In gym class. But ..." I glanced away. I really didn't want to go into this here and now. "I don't have the right equipment."

"That's the beauty of running. You don't need anything but sneakers, and I know you have those."

"Maybe that's true for men, but not for women. Particularly, um ..." My face turned red. "I need the right foundation garments. And I don't have them."

Liam frowned, and then understanding dawned. "Oh." He glanced down at my chest.

"Sorry." I couldn't meet his eyes.

"Hey, never apologize. Not for ...that." He licked his lips. "Don't they have special clothes for that? Like sports bras?"

"Well, yeah, but that's what I'm saying. I don't have any. Yoga pants are the extent of my sports-related clothes."

"You could get one."

"I could, but it's not the kind of thing they sell at the campus bookstore. Why is it such a big deal for me to run with you?"

He shrugged. "I don't know. I've got to keep up with my training, and it seemed like a way we could spend time together."

The idea that he wanted more time together made me happy in a giddy way. I still wasn't sold on the running idea, though.

"I was thinking of what you said about knowing me. Running is a big part of who I am. I wanted to share that with you." He stopped and turned toward me. "I need to go that way for class."

I reached up to touch his cheek. He must not have shaved that morning, because his beard rasped against my fingers.

"Thank you," I whispered. "For wanting to share that part of me with you."

He covered my fingers with his hand. "There're more parts I want to share with you."

"That's what friends do. They share stuff. Things they don't tell anyone else."

He grinned. "Some of what I want to share with you might go beyond the scope of friendship. How flexible are you about that?"

I hesitated. We'd been skirting close to and across the boundaries for the last week or so. It was only a matter of time before pretending that's all we were to each other would be ridiculous. I stood on tip-toe to kiss his cheek.

"I'm willing to explore that possibility." I winked and left him staring at me wide-eyed as I went back to the path that led to our dorm.

Julia was already in our room when I got back. I dropped my backpack into my closet and smiled at her.

"Hey, you feel like a shopping trip?"

"WHEN YOU SAID shopping, I thought you meant something fun." Julia sat on the bench in the fitting room, a pout on her face. "Like clothes or makeup or something like that. Not running bras."

"Sorry." I unclipped the first one from the hanger. "But thanks for coming. I really might need your help if I get stuck in one of these and can't get out."

"I still don't understand this sudden interest in running." She stretched her legs out in front of her as I pulled my top over my head and unhooked my bra.

"I don't know. It just seems like doing something physical wouldn't hurt me." I stuck my arms through the bra and gasped as I tried to pull it down. "Oh, my God, Jules, this isn't going to keep one boob still, let alone both of them."

"Here." She stood up and yanked on the back of the bra until it slipped into place. Unfortunately, it was the only thing that *was* in place; my boobs were sticking out both above and below. I stuffed them into the cups and checked out the mirror.

"Ugh. These things aren't designed for appeal, are they?" I stood sideways, not loving how the elastic squashed everything down. I hadn't looked this flat-chested since I was twelve years old.

"When you're running, you're not supposed to be worried about appeal." Julia's eyes narrowed. "Wait a minute. That's what this is about, isn't it? Liam. You're doing this for him."

I flushed. "No. I mean, I might run with him. Some time. I don't think there's anything wrong with running with a friend."

"Ava. Do you even hear yourself? I don't understand what you're doing."

I crossed my arms and struggled to pull off the bra. "I'm trying to find a decent sports bra because I have enormous boobs."

"That's not what I mean, and you know it. You're changing for a guy. And not even a decent guy. Liam Bai-

161

ley."

I finally got the elastic torture device off me. I re-attached it to the hanger and pulled down the next one. "Jules, I'm not changing for a guy. I'm just opening up new doors. Haven't you been telling me for the past three years that I need to try new things? Stop being so closed off and single-minded? Well, here I am. I thought you'd be happy."

"For anyone but Liam Bailey." She mumbled the words, hunched on the bench again.

"Aha." This one had a hook, which meant it was much easier to put on. "So Liam is the problem. Jules, please. I have this under control. Did you ever stop and think that maybe the Liam Bailey you knew was different than the one I know? Don't you remember how you guys fought all the time? You told me once if it hadn't been for Giff, you never would have stayed together as long as you did."

She nodded.

"It's not like with us. He ...he does things to make me happy. He's interested in what I like. We talk, and it's good. Please, Julia. I don't want this to come between us. I love you, and I always will." This was an awkward conversation to be having while trying on bras. "But this thing with Liam ...I don't know where it's going. Maybe nowhere. Maybe we'll just be friends. But I don't want to have to justify everything to you."

I turned to the mirror. "Well, more oomph, but not enough support. I'd give myself two black eyes running in this one." I glanced at Julia, and to my shock, she was crying.

"I'm sorry, Ave." She fumbled in her purse for a tissue. "I know I've been awful. I do want you to be happy. And I'm not jealous. I love Jesse. I'm *in* love with him. I know we're meant to be together. I guess I just feel like

...what was wrong with me that Liam didn't treat me like he does you? I see the look in his eyes when he watches you. He never cared about me. Not like that."

I hung up bra number two and began the torture of number three. "I don't know, Jules. Maybe it's a matter of who we're meant to be with. Jesse is such a perfect fit for you. I see you two together, and I can't imagine either of you ever being with anyone else. He worships the ground you walk on, like my mom says. And you get all glowy and bright around him. Whether you know it or not, you made me see that I want that. I want to find the person who makes me glowy. Maybe it's Liam. Maybe it's not. But I'm actually thinking about it now. That's a step, right?"

I got the bra on and tucked in my boobs. This one felt good: it had support, and yet it still let me have a little shape. I spun toward Jules, smiling.

"Ding, ding, I think we have a winner."

She wiped at her face and launched herself to me for a hug. "I think we do, too."

Laughing, I pushed at her. "Jules, I'm half-naked here in the dressing room. Seriously. Awkward."

"Sorry." She sat back down. "It just feels like everything is changing. I guess part of me thought there were a few things I could always depend on, like you sticking to your life plan and Liam being a dick. Now you're buying running bras and Liam's ..." She sighed. "I'm not ready to relinquish the dick part, but I guess as long as he's treating you well, I can keep my mouth shut."

"Thanks. Now can you help get me out of this thing? I think I'm stuck."

JULIA AND I ate dinner in the food court at the mall, and then I dropped her back at the dorm before I rushed off to make the RA council meeting. These were generally a waste of time, mostly consisting of people bitching about the students in their dorms or the leaders showing us long and pointless presentations on methods of coping with young college students. I sat in the back with a notebook that was actually from my Cognition class. I was behind in reviewing my notes there.

"Hey, peaches. Is this fun or what?"

I looked up as Giff slid into the chair next to me. He was wearing chinos and dress shirt, and I raised an eyebrow.

"Aren't you a little dressed up for a council meeting?" Giff always looked good, but he was also savvy about the right clothes for any occasion. Nice shorts and a shirt would have been typical for this kind of evening.

He made a face. "Yeah, well, I didn't have time to change after dinner."

"Jeff take you out some place fancy?"

"I wish. No, I went to dinner with Liam and his parents. Always a fun-fest with those three."

My stomach fell. "Liam's parents are here?"

Giff flipped open his tablet. "Yeah. I guess it was a last minute deal. Believe me, it wasn't a pleasure cruise tonight. I've been playing buffer between them for a long time, but the last few months ..." He shook his head. "I needed a drink. Or three."

I shifted. "Liam didn't tell me they were coming today."

"Oh, don't be mad about that. Trust me, he was protecting you."

I snorted. "Or he just didn't think I was important

enough to meet them."

The meeting began, and Giff lowered his voice, leaning toward me.

"Peaches, that's not it. Don't go making this into a big deal."

"But it is a big deal, Giff. He practically strong-armed me into taking him to meet my parents this weekend. And yet his are right here, and he can't invite me to dinner?"

Giff heaved a sigh. "It's so much more complicated than that."

"Yeah, there's that word again. *Complicated.* I'm beginning to think it's Liam's middle name."

"This time it's for real. He told me about being with you over the weekend. He thinks your family is amazing. But his parents aren't like that. He's probably afraid they'd eat you alive."

"I'm a big girl, Giff. I can handle them."

"Maybe, but try to understand. Liam doesn't want you to get hurt."

The girl in front of us turned around and shot us a dirty look. I guessed we were distracting her from the fascinating presentation on helping freshmen transition to sophomore year.

I pulled out my phone and texted Liam.

Hey. How was your night?

I propped the phone on the edge of the desk, watching for Liam's response. There was nothing for a long time, and then it was just one word.

Hell.

I waited, but there was nothing more, so I typed another question.

Are you okay?

This time, the answer was faster.

No.

I bit the side of my lip, thinking. I wasn't sure if there was anything I could do to help him, but sitting here while Liam was hurting was a waste of time.

I put my mouth close to Giff's ear. "Was Liam in your room?"

He shook his head and whispered back to me. "I left from the restaurant since I had this meeting. But they were about to head out, too, I think. Why?"

I shut my notebook and shoved it into my bag. "I'm going to check on him."

Giff grabbed my arm. "Hey, peaches, I'm not sure that's a good idea. Liam ...after a visit with his parents, he needs some time to decompress. You should give him space tonight. Leave him alone."

I hesitated. I wasn't Liam's girlfriend, not really. I was his friend, and maybe a little more than that. But would showing up uninvited tonight be pushing? I tried to imagine what he would do if our positions were reversed. It wasn't even a question; I knew he'd be there for me, whether I asked him or not. Whether I wanted him or not.

"Are you going back to the dorm after the meeting?" I leaned nearer Giff again.

He glanced at me. "No. I'm going right to Jeff's from here. But I think—"

I stood up, grabbing my bag. "Thanks, Giff." I kissed him on the cheek. "You're a good friend. Don't worry, I know what I'm doing."

God, I hoped I did.

Chapter Thirteen

THE WALK TO the dorm where Liam and Giff lived only took me a few minutes. The night was warm, with just a hint of chill in the air, but I didn't linger to enjoy it. A sense of urgency beat within my chest. Maybe I was fool, but if Liam needed me ...

I clenched my fingers. That was the question. Did he need me? He hadn't bothered to let me know he was seeing his parents tonight, and he hadn't thought to invite me to join them. Maybe I was fooling myself. Maybe I was going to get up to his room, and he'd wonder why I'd come. Why I'd forced myself into a situation where I wasn't wanted. Or needed.

I took a deep breath and turned into the building. Their room was on the first floor, and I only had to turn one corner before I was standing in front of their door.

This was it. I could still turn around and walk away right now, and Liam would never know. I could pretend that I'd gone straight back to my own room, and tomorrow morning, I would act as though Giff hadn't told me anything.

Or I could knock at the door, knowing this was a turning point. If I went in and Liam did need me, if I could offer him any comfort ...I would be committing to more than friendship. I knew I'd been kidding myself for a while anyway; we both knew the friendship pact was just a cover for what Liam wanted. For what, maybe, both of us wanted.

I lifted my hand and knocked.

I thought I heard a sound from within, but there was no answer. I swallowed and paused with my hand on the doorknob. If it were locked, I had my answer. I would go back to my room.

I turned it, and the door opened.

The room was dark; only the campus street lights let me see the outline of furniture. I stood for a minute, letting my eyes adjust as I scanned the room. I saw the two empty beds and desks with books and papers. Giff's chair was pulled out, and a t-shirt hung over the back of it.

Liam wasn't here. A wave that was a mix of disappointment and relief swept over me. I closed my eyes and berated myself: what had I expected? That I was going to come in and fix whatever might be wrong with him? I was an idiot.

I turned around and stumbled over something. Grabbing onto the bookcase was the only thing that kept me from landing on the floor next to ...Liam.

He was sitting propped up against his bed, shadowed so that I hadn't seen him before. His head lolled back against the side of the mattress. I knelt down alongside his legs, and my hand hit the cold of a glass bottle. I couldn't see the label in the dark, but I had a pretty good idea of what it would say judging from the smell coming off him.

"Liam." I touched his face, turned it to me. His eyes fluttered opened, staring at me unfocused. And then he groaned.

"Hey." I trailed a finger down his jaw. "It's me."

"Ava?" His voice was rough.

"Yeah. I'm right here."

His hand rose to cup my cheek. "I was dreaming of you."

I smiled as warmth spread over me. "Really? What was I doing?"

"This." He put a little pressure on the back of my neck and pulled me to his lips. His breath was heavy with the smell of whiskey, but I didn't even pause. I opened my mouth, letting his tongue plunder me thoroughly. My breasts pressed into his chest, and I wriggled against him.

"God, Ava. My God, I want you." He slid his free hand under my shirt between us, palming my breast. I gasped against his mouth.

"Liam." I wanted, too. Good God, how I wanted. But I pulled back, leaning on his shoulders. "Hey. We need to talk."

He groaned. "I had enough talk tonight. I just want you."

"Why didn't you tell me your parents were coming?"

He dropped his head back. "Giff?"

"Yeah."

He blew out a breath. "Sorry. I wasn't trying to hide it. They're ...Ava, my parents are not like yours. The idea of letting them get in the middle of whatever it is we have ...they'd make it ugly."

I frowned. "I'm sure it's not that bad."

He laughed, but there was no humor in it. "Trust me, sweetheart. It's worse."

"Tell me about it."

"No. I don't want to talk about them. I want to be with you. Stay with me tonight, Ava. Let me make you feel good."

I pressed my lips together and brushed the hair out of Liam's eyes. "I'll stay. But I want you to tell me what happened with your parents that made you come back and drink yourself to oblivion."

He stretched his neck. "I'm not that drunk, Ava. Just slightly numb."

"I'm glad to hear it." I settled alongside him, sitting on the floor with his arm over my shoulders. "Then you can talk."

He sighed. "You're not going to let this go, are you?"

"Nope."

"Hmmm." He ran his hand down my hair. "So you came over here after Giff told you about our dinner?"

"I was worried about you."

"You're a good friend." He nuzzled my neck.

"I think we both know the friendship train jumped the track a long time ago. At least, I think it did."

"Yeah. So where does that leave us?"

I smiled and laced my fingers into his. "We'll figure it out. But first ...tell me about tonight. Nice try on the distraction, though. You get an A for effort."

"Thanks." He swallowed and tightened his hold on my hand. "I told you my mom and dad aren't like yours. But we used to be able to at least talk. They listened to me. Then a few months back, everything changed."

"What happened? What made them change?"

He shook his head. "Not them. Me. I'm the one who's different now."

I frowned. "Okay. How? And why?"

He was quiet, and his arm snuggled me closer to him. "Ava, I've never talked to anyone about this. Not Giff. Not anyone."

I felt the rebuff. "All right." I started to push up and

away. "I understand. I know you're private—"

"No, you don't understand." He pulled me back. "I'm not saying I won't tell you. Just that it's hard."

I sat back down, facing Liam on my knees. After a moment, I slid one leg over top of his so that I straddled his lap. His head jerked up to look at me.

"Watch me." I leaned down to kiss the side of his neck. "I'm right here. I'm not leaving. You can tell me anything, and I'll still be here."

He ran his hands up my arms. "You ...you amaze me." He took a deep breath and looked into my eyes as he began to speak.

"Remember the night you asked me why I had broken up with Julia like I did? I said it was complicated, and it was. A lot more than I could tell anyone." He traced one finger up to my shoulder, making me shiver.

"We had dinner together one night, my parents, Giff and Julia. My dad talked about all the events coming up that I was expected to attend, and he told Julia that he hoped she'd come along on one of them. A big one. And it shouldn't have mattered, but something hit me. My father was talking like he expected Julia to be around for a while, and that made me panic.

"I started to think about what I wanted, and I realized it wasn't Julia. I know that sounds bad, but for the first time, I was seeing things more clearly. So I went to talk to my father. I drove up to the house on a Thursday afternoon, just to let him know I was planning to tell Julia I thought we should break up. I wanted his advice. Maybe his approval. His car was in the driveway, and I called for him when I walked in, but I didn't see him in his library or office. I thought I heard a sound upstairs, so I went to check." He swallowed, hard. "He was there. But he wasn't alone. He was in bed with a woman I'd never seen before."

"Oh, Liam," I breathed. "God. I'm sorry."

He went on as though I hadn't spoken. "I went out, but he had seen me. I drove back to school, and I went for a run. Just to get away. And he was in my room when I got back. He'd sent Giff away, told him we needed to have a private conversation. I told him I didn't want to hear anything he had to say, and my father told me it was time I understood the facts of life."

There was derision in his voice. I rocked forward and held his face, stroked down his cheeks. They were wet.

"He wanted me to know that he loved my mother. In his way. That they were comfortable, and she was a good political wife. He said he'd never do anything to embarrass her, and that I had to understand there were ..." He closed his eyes. "Girls you married and girls you fucked. Julia, according to him, was one of the marrying kind. She would be a good asset to me.

"I told him it didn't matter, I was about to break up with her, and he told me that would be stupid. He said if she wasn't giving me what I needed, I could always get it elsewhere."

Everything was beginning to fall into place. "That was right before your birthday, wasn't it?"

He nodded. "Yeah. I didn't plan to do it that way. But the night of the party, it felt like the walls were closing in. Like ...if I didn't make a change, and fast, I was going to be stuck in my father's life. The idea of that made me sick, and it made me do something terrible to someone who didn't deserve it."

Liam's jaw clenched, and he stared over my shoulder. "So that's the truth. And since that night, everything with my parents has been ...strained. I can't look at my mother without seeing my father in bed with that woman. And I don't want to hear anything my father says. I haven't been home since Christmas, and I tell them I'm busy whenever they come down. They surprised me tonight. I didn't know they were going to be here when I saw you this afternoon. I got back after track practice, and they were here. I roped Giff into going to dinner with us."

He reached up to frame my face in his hands. "You have to believe, it wasn't that I didn't want them to know about you. About us. It just wasn't the time."

I studied his blue eyes. He was watching me, gauging my reaction. I leaned forward and touched my lips to his, joining our mouths in a promise of understanding.

"Okay."

Liam raised his eyes to me. "Okay?"

"Yes. I get it. I understand. And I don't want to be someone who makes your relationship with your parents more ..." I smiled. "Complicated. Sorry, I couldn't resist."

"You wouldn't. You don't complicate anything, Ava. When I'm with you, everything feels so much clearer and simpler."

"I feel the same way." I laid down flat, with my ear on his chest so I could hear the beating of his heart. "I thought you were bringing all kinds of mess to my life, screwing up my perfect plan. But now ..." I turned my head so that my chin rested on his sternum. "The plan feels kind of empty if you're not part of it."

Liam moved his hands to my sides and pulled me up along his body until my face was even with his. "Does this mean the friendship rules are off the table?"

I nodded. "Not that you ever paid any attention to them, anyway."

"But now I can do this without worrying about having to feel guilty or making explanations later."

He pressed my mouth into his, and if I'd thought he'd

kissed me with passion before, I was wrong. So, so wrong. Now he branded me, claiming me with his lips and tongue and teeth. His mouth opened and coaxed mine to do the same, as he swallowed the hum of satisfaction and need that came from my throat.

The tip of his tongue ran over the inside of my lips, and I shivered. And then he plunged deep within my mouth, tangling and stroking. His hands rubbed slow circles up and down my sides, coming closer and closer to the sides of my breasts each time.

I sat up, bringing my knees up along his hips and settling my center more fully over the straining I felt through his khakis. Liam sucked in a deep breath as I rocked, and he brought his hands down to grip my ass.

"You feel good," I whispered, leaning my hands on his chest.

"God, you have no idea." He moved his hands to my boobs, cupping them through my shirt. His thumbs stroked my nipples, and even through two layers, I thought I was going to burst into flames. I reached for the hem of my shirt and pulled it over my head.

Liam's eyes widened as he took me in. "You are so fucking beautiful, Ava." His hands came up to trace over the lace of my bra. "Let me make you feel good."

He slipped his fingers under the cup and eased it down and then leaned forward, capturing my nipple in his mouth. He sucked hard and then caught it between his teeth. His tongue joined in, pressing the tip to the roof of his mouth. I moaned and felt his lips move into a smile.

"Is that a good moan?"

I hissed in a breath. "It's a for-the-love-of-God-don't-stop moan."

"Not planning on it." He caught the stiff peak between his teeth again, and at the same time his hand found the other nipple, pinching it through the lace between finger and thumb. I arched forward and clutched at his back, holding us together.

"Ava." He rained kisses between my breasts, up to my neck. "I'm going to make you come. I'm going to touch you everywhere. But I'm not going to make love to you tonight. When we do ...I want it to be ...untouched by anything else. Not because I'm mad about my parents. Or anything else. Just you. Just me. Okay?"

I blinked back tears that took me by surprise. "Thank you."

He darted his tongue into my ear, sucked the lobe into his mouth. "For what? I haven't done anything yet."

"For being the most wonderful man I've ever met. For caring about me. For protecting me." I turned my head to meet his mouth, pouring everything I felt into our kiss.

"Always." Liam reached behind my back to unhook my bra. The straps slid down my arms and he tossed it to the side. His mouth feasted on me as I held his head and rubbed the throbbing need at my center to the bulge below me.

He slid his hands down the front of my pants, his fingers skimming over the top of my panties. My position kept him from reaching me, and he growled.

"Lift up." I obeyed without hesitation, and Liam worked the button and zipper on my pants. Between the two of us, we wiggled them down, and I kicked them off. Liam wasted no time in bringing his fingers between my legs, running them over my inner thighs and then finally, finally touching me over the cloth of my underwear.

I rocked closer, moaning in short bursts. Pleasure was building, and everything in my world was centered on his fingers as they stroked me.

"You're so hot, baby. I want to see you come, and I

want to hear you say my name when you do."

"God—Liam—"

He pushed the material out of the way, and his fingers slid inside me. I gripped his shirt, holding myself up on his chest, staring into the blue eyes that threatened to set me ablaze.

"Come on, Ava. Let it go. Look at me. Let me watch you." His thumb moved up to press against the small bundle of nerves that craved his touch and I shot straight up, his name the only word on my lips and the only thought in my head.

"Liam!"

Every inch of my body sizzled with a bolt of pleasure, so deep and so intense that I didn't think I could breathe. I arched backward, my eyes closing in spite of myself.

I fell forward, collapsing on Liam. "My God. Oh, my God. Liam."

His hand rubbed over my back. "I'm right here." He tilted my chin up to touch my lips with his. "I'll always be right here."

W E FELL ASLEEP there on the floor. At some point, Liam lifted me with him to his bed, and when I woke, I was tucked with my back against his front. His arms circled me, and my head was below his chin.

I blinked slowly against the light streaming in from the windows. I couldn't tell what time it was, but I was pretty certain I'd already slept through one class. My phone was in my bag, somewhere on the floor along with my clothes. I could have wiggled loose and retrieved it, but the thought of moving right now was not appealing.

"Waking up with you is the second-best thing I've ever experienced." Liam's voice was low and husky in my ear. I smiled and nestled closer.

"Only second-best? What's the first?"

"Watching you come while I touch you. Hearing you say my name when you fall apart."

I sighed, my eyes drifting shut again. "Yeah, that was way up there on my list, too."

"I think we're going to be late for class this morning."

"Do you care?"

He laughed, pulled me tighter. "No, but I thought you might be freaking out about it."

I shrugged. "Nah. I don't ever miss, so I figure I've built up a pretty good credibility account with my professors. One day isn't going to kill me." A small pang of panic grabbed at my heart, but I tamped it down.

"I like that way of thinking." He kissed the top of my head.

"Liam ...about last night."

"Yeah?" I felt his arms tense, and I ran my fingers over his hands to relax him.

"No, not that part of last night. I don't have regrets. I mean ...what you told me about your parents. You need to tell Julia. You need to explain things to her."

He blew out a sigh. "Why? It's over. It's done, and I've apologized and we've both moved on. Why should I drag the whole thing back up now?"

"Because Julia needs to know. You apologized, yes, but you never explained. It will make a difference to her." I turned in his arms so I could look into his eyes. "And to us. I don't want what you and I have to get in between my friendship with Jules. She's important to me."

Liam smoothed his thumb over my cheekbone, his eyes studying me. "You have the most beautiful skin, you know that? It's like what Giff calls you ...peaches and cream. I always wondered if it were the same all over your body. It is."

I felt a blush creep over my cheeks. "Thanks, but you're not going to distract me. Will you talk to her?"

He closed his eyes. "Okay. If it's important to you, I will."

"Thank you." I kissed his chin. "Now as much as I want to stay right here with you, I better get moving. Speaking of Julia, she's probably freaking out that I didn't come home last night." I started to sit up and then paused. "Turn over."

Liam narrowed his eyes. "Why?"

"Because I'm naked. I need to get my clothes."

He laughed as his arm snaked around to grab me again. "Ava, I don't want to point out the obvious, but I've seen you naked now. I saw you last night, sitting on me naked. And I slept with you all night, naked."

"I know, but now it's daylight, and it's morning, and I'm going to have to bend over to get my stuff. I'm not ready for that yet. Call me a prude, but it's how I am."

Still laughing, Liam rolled over so that his back faced me. "All right. Tell me when it's safe to open my eyes."

I darted off the bed, keeping my gaze on the bed to make sure he didn't peek. I pulled on my underwear and jeans first, and then hooked my bra. "It's safe to look."

Liam turned back, raising one eyebrow when he saw me. "So it's okay for me to see you in just your bra?"

"Baby steps. For me, I mean. I'm comfortable with you seeing me like this." I sat down on the edge of the bed. "And I wanted to give you something to remember all day. Just a little reminder."

"That's more than a little reminder. That's something that's going to make it impossible to sit through my classes today."

I leaned over to drop a quick kiss on his mouth before I stood up. "You're welcome."

Ch♥pter Fourteen

AS IT TURNED out, Julia had figured out where I was on her own. She had texted me twice, and then she'd called Giff, who had told her I was with Liam.

"If you're going to spend the night with him, you need to tell me." She sat on her bed, her arms crossed. "Because I was worried. I was this close to calling your mom."

"That threat is losing power." I stuck my tongue out at her as I dug for clean clothes. "I really am sorry. I ...we got involved. And then we fell asleep and it was too late. It was complicated."

"It always is, with Liam."

I closed my dresser drawer. "Jules, Liam needs to talk to you about something, Will you hear him out, please? For me?"

She stared at me for a minute. "What does he want to talk about?"

"About the night of his birthday party." When she rolled her eyes, I held up my hand. "Please, Julia. It's important for all of us that he can tell you what happened. Okay?"

Finally Julia nodded. "I'll listen. I'm not promising anything else."

I crossed the room to give her a swift hug. "Thanks. That's all I can ask."

They met that afternoon at Beans. I stayed away on purpose, knowing that this had to be between the two of them only. Julia came back to the dorm by herself an hour later.

She met my eyes. "He told me. Everything, I mean." She dropped onto her bed. "It makes me want to call my parents and thank them for not screwing me up like that. God, Ava. I knew they were kind of stiff and formal, but this is crazy."

"Do you feel any better about the whole situation?"

She sighed. "I guess so. I mean, at least now I understand why he acted that way. He didn't use it as an excuse. He told me he knew he fucked up—his words, not mine—and that he was sorry I was the one who took the brunt of it."

I closed my eyes, nodding. "Good."

"Ava." When I looked up, Julia was looking at me with worry in her eyes. "Are you sure about this whole thing with Liam? I thought I was okay with it, and I am, really. But I'm not sure it's the best thing for you. His parents are going to be a problem."

"Why would they be?"

She shook her head. "It's just how they are. Their circle of friends is small and tight. I was okay to date Liam, but just barely, I think. I don't want you to be hurt. Maybe you should stop and think before you get too deeply involved."

One corner of my mouth lifted in a half-smile. "I think it's too late, Jules."

SINCE I'D NEVER been in a romantic relationship in college—or ever, really—learning to adjust over the next few weeks was interesting. I'd seen how Liam had been with Julia, but if I'd expected the same thing with me, I'd have been very mistaken.

He texted me first thing every morning, and last thing before he went to sleep at night, even if we'd been together all day. We met for lunch on the days that our schedules allowed it, and we ate dinner together just about every night, unless the track team was traveling.

I went to all of his track meets, and if it was annoying to hear girls around me sighing over how sexy Liam Bailey was, knowing that after everything was over, it was me he'd meet at the fence for a searing kiss made it all better.

His parents hadn't been back down to Birch since the night he'd told me everything, and Liam seemed to be relieved by that. We were getting ready for our weekend trip to Carl and Angela's wedding, and I was pretty sure Liam was more nervous about it than I was.

My mother called me on the Tuesday before the wedding. I was walking back to the dorm after class, listening more than talking as she filled me in on everything that had been happening. All I had to do was make the appropriate listening noises every few minutes.

"Yeah, Ma. Uh-huh. Oh, really? Wow." I dodged a guy who was heading in the opposite direction. "I'm sure. Yeah. Oh!"

The last exclamation was courtesy of the arm that gripped me around the waist, hauling me off the path.

"Hasn't anyone ever warned you about big bad

wolves, Red?" Liam's voice tickled in my ear.

"No, Ma, sorry, that's just—" I shot him a look and pointed at my phone. "I'm walking back from class. Go ahead. What about the flowers?"

"This big bad wolf has big bad plans for you." Liam lifted my hair from the side of my neck where I wasn't holding the phone and began kissing down my jaw. His tongue drew tantalizing designs on my skin. I closed my eyes and tried to breathe.

"Yeah. No, I don't blame you. Isn't Angela's family—ahhhh."

Liam's hands were inching up my ribs, teasing the undersides of my breasts. I made a face at him.

"No, Ma. It's fine. Any time. Okay. Love to Daddy. Okay. Love you. Bye." I hit the end button on my phone and turned to face Liam. "Geez—I was talking to my mother!"

"Mmmm-hmmm." He kissed me, this time on the lips, nudging at my closed lips with his tongue.

"I was about to start moaning into the telephone. That would have been fun to explain." I smoothed my fingers over his jaw. "What are you doing out here, anyway?"

"Just stalking any innocent young thing walking on the path." He grabbed my ass and brought me close.

"Don't you have a class right now?" I'd gotten to know his schedule pretty well.

"I do, but it was canceled." He slung an arm over my shoulder as we began walking to the dorms.

"Cool. So what are you going to do this afternoon?"

"I was thinking of going for a run, and then taking my girlfriend out to dinner."

I stopped abruptly in the path, looking up at him in mock indignation. "Wait a minute—you have a girlfriend? Then why were you kissing me?"

He winked. "My girlfriend is very understanding. She's also really beautiful, so she knows I never look at anyone but her. She's smart, she's gorgeous, and she's got a killer body."

I felt my face pinking. "Seriously? She sounds like quite a package."

"Oh, she is. She's got it all. Sometimes I don't know what she sees in a loser like me. I don't deserve her."

I stood on my toes. "Maybe she knows you're intelligent, kind, funny and not bad looking. Maybe she wonders what she ever did to deserve you."

"Not bad looking, huh? Is that the best you can do?"

"If I said anything else, your ego would be too inflated." I threaded our hands together and began walking again. "So ...do you want company on your run?"

Liam raised his eyebrows. "What do you mean? You? I thought you didn't run."

"I don't, but I'm willing to try. I even bought the necessary equipment. If you want me to come with you, I mean. If you want to be by yourself, I understand."

He leaned over to kiss the top of my head. "I would never choose being alone over being with you." He pulled out his phone to check the time. "I'll meet you right outside your building in fifteen minutes. That enough time?"

"It should be. As long Julia is there to help me get into my running bra. The thing is like a torture device."

"Well, if she's not there, let me know. I'm always happy to help. Bras are my specialty."

"Thanks. You're so helpful."

I dashed up the steps to my room and dropped my backpack into the closet. Julia was just getting ready to go to work.

"Hey, glad I saw you. I'm going to stay after with Jesse tonight. His mom is in town." She rolled her eyes.

"Ewwww. Well, you have fun with that. I'm going for a run with Liam. Wish me luck."

She laughed. "Good luck. Don't break a leg or anything else vital."

I pulled on running shorts and then tackled the sports bra. I managed to get it over my head and most of the way down by myself, and Julia gave it a final tug.

"I think you're set now, but you're probably going to need help to get it off." She picked up her bag to leave.

I grinned. "If I play my cards right, that won't be an issue."

Julia covered her ears. "Yuck! TMI. My ears."

"Yeah, whatever. Have fun tonight."

I laced up my sneakers, picked up my sunglasses and locked the door behind me before I went down to meet Liam. He was standing by the bench, stretching his hamstrings.

He looked up as I approached, and his eyebrows shot up. "Wow. Look at you."

I glanced down. "What? Don't I look like a runner?"

He smiled. "You look perfect. Come on. I'll take it slow on you today. We don't have to go that far."

We took off down the brick path. I was surprised at how well the bra worked; nothing bounced on me at all. It was oddly freeing. Maybe I could be a runner after all.

We circled the campus twice before Liam began to slow down. He wasn't even out of breath, but I was panting.

"You did great." He pulled me over to a wooden bench that was set back in the trees. I collapsed onto it.

"Yeah, I think I slowed you down. You're incredible." I ranged my eyes over his smooth back, tight rear end and his toned legs. Thinking of how his arms looked when he held himself above me made wish we were some place much more private.

"You didn't slow me down. It was fun. Nice to have someone to enjoy the run with." He took my hand, bringing my knuckles to his lips. "Thank you."

I leaned to rest my head on his shoulder. "No, thank you."

We sat in the quiet, enjoying the chirping of the birds and cool of the air over our sweaty bodies.

"Ava, can I ask you something?"

"Of course you can."

He fiddled with the lace of his shoe. "Are you a virgin?"

The bottom fell out of my stomach. I figured this would come up, but I hadn't expected it now. I swallowed over a lump in my throat.

"No, I'm not."

I felt his start of surprise. "I thought you didn't date. I mean, you always said—"

"I know." I bit my lip. "It happened in high school."

"Was it your boyfriend? You never mentioned having one."

"No, I didn't. Not really." I released a breath. "After Antonia got pregnant and had Frankie, everything in my family was kind of ...messed up. I mean, everyone was so preoccupied with her and what was going on, I fell under the radar. Except that every now and then, my mom would pull me aside and tell me that I had to let Antonia be a lesson to me, that if a good girl like her could get in trouble, it could happen to anyone. And since she wasn't going to be able to go to college like they'd planned, now all the expectation fell on me."

"Whew." Liam smoothed my hair away from my face. "That's rough."

"Yeah, only they didn't mean anything by it. They

were doing the best they could under the circumstances. So anyway, one night when Frankie was seven months old, I went to a party. I was sick of being home with Antonia and the baby, helping with everything, working at the restaurant, doing homework ...it just felt like I had no life. So I went to the party, and I met this guy I'd been flirting with in math. He was cute, and he was nice, and he paid attention to me. One thing led to another, and we ended up in one of the bedrooms upstairs."

"Bastard."

I shook my head. "No, Liam, he didn't force me. If I had stopped us at any time, he'd have been fine. I knew what I was doing. But then after, I came downstairs, and my friends said they'd been looking for me. My mom had called, and I needed to get home right away." I closed my eyes, remembering. "Antonia had run out to get diapers, and she was hit head-on by a drunk driver. She died instantly."

Liam pulled me into him. He held my face in his hands and used his thumbs to wipe away tears I hadn't known I'd been crying.

"I'm so sorry, Ava."

I sniffed. "So the next day, I made a decision. I felt like ...what happened to Antonia was punishment. I mean, I know God doesn't work that way. No one would've ever taught me that. But I made a promise to Antonia that I'd stick to the path. I'd work hard, and I'd go to college and get the big job and I wouldn't let any boy or anything else get in the way."

"And so was born the plan."

"Yep." I nodded. "That was it. And it was working out just fine, until you came along." I bumped him with my shoulder.

"I'd say I'm sorry, but I'm not. Ava, you know, I don't

want to take you off your path. But I'd like to think we can walk our paths together." He grimaced. "That sounded corny."

"It did, but I happen to love it." I kissed his cheek. "I'd be lying if I didn't say I still have panic attacks about easing up. About having a life, instead of just having a plan. But I can't imagine being without you."

Liam lifted me so that I lay across his lap, with my head resting on his shoulder. "You know the nice thing about running together? We're both sweaty. So I can kiss you and touch you without worrying that I'm being gross."

He started out with a light kiss, just a gentle caress of my lips with his. I dug my fingers in his shoulders, needing more, and he obliged, opening his mouth and licking at the insides of my lips. I moaned, and he hiked me closer, sliding his hand under my tank top to where my breasts usually were.

"God, what is this?"

"I told you, it's a running bra." I spoke against his mouth. "It keeps everything flat. No jiggling. I may start wearing it all the time now, so I don't have to worry about bouncing around."

"Ah, no." Liam shook his head. "I like the jiggle. I love your breasts. Matter of fact, I love every inch of your body." He laid one hand along my cheek and looked down into my eyes, serious all at once. "I would like to take you up to my room and show you just how much."

I understood what he was saying, what he was asking me. It was a point of no turning back, although, if I were to be honest, I'd passed that point long ago.

"Yes." I breathed the word. "Yes, please."

I WAS STRANGELY calm as Liam locked the door behind us. He seemed to have enough nerves for us both.

"You're sure Giff isn't coming back?" I had to ask one more time as I toed off my sneakers and tucked my socks into them.

"Positive. He's staying at Jeff's." Liam was doing the same with his shoes.

"Okay." I smiled into his eyes and grabbed the hem of my tank, pulling it over my head.

"Ava, if you're not sure about this, you know we don't have to do it."

"Liam." I laid my hand on his arm. "I'm sure." I reached for his shirt, running my hands underneath to trace his abs. "Take this off, please."

"Yes, ma'am." He stripped it over his head, tossed it into a basket by the wall and stepped toward me. "Better?"

"Any time you have your shirt off, it's all good." I ran my hands over his muscled torso. Being free to touch him any time I wanted was one of my favorite perks of being Liam's girlfriend.

"Funny, I feel the same about you." He wrapped his arms around me and walked me backwards until my knees bumped into the bed. I sank down, and Liam knelt in front of me.

Taking my face between his hands, he began kissing me, starting at my eyes and moving down to the corner of my mouth. Before he moved to cover my lips, he paused.

"The first time I touched my lips to yours, I realized I hadn't been alive until that minute. I'd been existing." He angled his head and slanted his mouth, nudging mine open. I made a small mewling noise, and he lowered me back onto the mattress. He stroked my mouth with his tongue, and then sucked mine into his mouth. When he broke the connection, I was dizzy with want.

"I think it's time to get rid of this." He traced a finger over the running bra, and then worked on easing the straps down my arms. Frowning when it stuck, he pulled a little harder.

"I told you it's not easy," I giggled.

"It won't defeat me." He abandoned the straps and instead, tugged down the cup. My boob sprang free, pushed upward by the elastic. Liam grinned.

"I take it back, I think I like this thing." He dipped his head to lick the sensitive areole, teasing all around the pink nub until I was breathless again.

"What is it? Tell me what you want."

I moaned and tried to move his head into the right place.

"Use your words. What do you need, Ava?"

I gritted my teeth. "I want you to—to suck my nipple."

Liam smiled against my breast and immediately complied. I moaned again, this time in satisfaction. He swirled his tongue around the peak, worried it between his teeth and sucked it gently. His hand moved to the other side, slipping under the edge and freeing it as well.

Pleasure coursed through me as he lavished attention on my breasts. I ran my hands down his back and then slid my fingers beneath the waistband of his shorts to feel the smooth skin of his ass. He growled, deep in his throat, and looked up at me.

With a smile I could only call promising, he began kissing down my ribs, across my stomach, stopping to dip his tongue into my navel. When he reached my running shorts, he grasped them with both hands and pulled down, baring me completely.

It was the first time we'd been together in daylight,

and part of me wanted to push him away, hide myself. The other part of me was too busy groaning in utter ecstasy. I decided to go with her, and I parted my legs as Liam lowered his face between them. He opened me with his fingers and ran one finger down my seam. I gasped and arched my back.

"Shhh, baby, take it slow." He used the pad of his thumb to massage my clit, and I clutched a handful of sheets below me, my breath coming in short bursts.

"Liam—oh, my God—" He covered me with his mouth, his tongue first replacing his thumb and then stabbing into me, over and over until I fell completely apart, gasping his name as I held his head. Colors exploded before my eyes, and every single nerve in my body was pulsing with pleasure.

He kissed back up my stomach and lifted my boneless legs onto the bed. When he lay down next to me, he managed to get his fingers under the tight band at the bottom of my bra.

"We're getting this off you now. Sit up a little."

I swiveled my head to look at him. "I don't think I can."

He grinned. "That good, huh? Well, just a little." He kissed the side of my ear. "When I'm inside you, I want you completely naked, and I want to hold your tits in my hand."

I remembered the night we'd gone out to dinner, when I'd worn the black skirt. *At this minute, all I can think is that I want to back you into the wall, lift up that skirt and drive into you. Wrap your gorgeous legs around my waist, with your heels still on, so I can feel them against my back. Fill my hands with your tits, suck your nipples into my mouth. Pound myself inside you until you come so loud and hard, you scream my name loud enough for the whole building to hear.*

I giggled and leaned up. Liam pulled hard enough that the bra finally flew off, over my head.

"What?" He raised an eyebrow.

"I was thinking that I want to wear my black skirt and heels again, soon."

"Oh, my God, Ava, you're going to kill me." He palmed my boobs, his eyes dark and smoldering. "Never complain about the jiggle, baby. I fucking love your tits." He bent his head over them again.

I used his distraction to reach down between us and touch him through the thin nylon of his running shorts. He hissed in a breath, but he didn't move. I smiled and stroked his length with steady fingers.

"I want to touch you," I murmured into his ear as he held himself above me.

"I thought you were."

"No, I want to touch you without ...these." I pulled at the shorts.

"That can definitely be arranged." Liam slid off the shorts, kicking them to the floor, and a brand new desire shot through me at the sight of him, jutting out hard and long. I grasped him and moved my fist up and down, but I was having trouble reaching everything I wanted to reach.

"Flip over." I pushed at his shoulder.

"Why?" He kissed the valley between my breasts.

"Just do it. I promise, I'll make it worth your while."

Grinning, he flipped to his back. I sat up next to him and eased one leg over until I straddled him.

"Okay, I like this." He reached up run his finger over my nipple.

"Stick around, you might find something else you enjoy, too." I bent over his chest and fastened my mouth on the flat disc of his nipple, curious about how it felt. Clearly it was a good move, because he groaned and rubbed the back of my head. I licked the circle and then moved to the other side, leaving my fingers on the first moist point, mimicking what Liam did to my breasts.

I reached below to take hold of his cock, trailing my fingers over it as I began to kiss down the center of his stomach.

"Ava, what are you doing?"

I sat up and smiled at him. "Whatever I want to do."

He caught my hand. "I want to come inside you. You don't have to do this."

I shook my head. "I know I don't *have* to. I want to try this. I want to ...feel every part of you. In every way."

Before he could say anything else, I lowered my mouth to take him in, experimenting with pressure and movement. I licked him, bringing my tongue in a circle, and then moved my mouth up and down the shaft. It gave me an unbelievable sense of power to do this, to feel his pleasure as he groaned my name.

"Ava, oh, my God, Ava. So. . so. . good." His hips began to thrust toward my mouth.

The need was building again between my legs. More than before, because now I wanted more than just pleasure. I wanted to be filled. I crawled up his body, and laying down half on top of him, whispered in his ear.

"Make love to me, Liam. I want you inside me. Please."

In an instant, he had flipped me back over, and leaning to the desk drawer, pulled out a small paper square. I sat up on my elbows to watch him roll on the condom. His eyes met mine, all fire and want, as he rose over me.

His lips crushed mine at the same moment that he nudged at my entrance. I cried out and lifted my hips, taking him deeper so that he was buried inside me. The muscles of his arms stood out in knotted tension as he thrust, deep and long and hard.

"Ava, my God, Ava—"

It took me a moment to get used to the feeling of him within me. He stretched me, and I moved a bit, experimenting with the sensation. When I arched up, he stroked against a spot that made me gasp. I gripped his ass to bring him in even tighter.

"Ava—baby—I don't know how long I can hold out." He was speaking through gritted teeth, barely holding onto control. I pulled his face down to kiss me.

"Then don't hold out."

I lifted my legs and wrapped them around his waist, calling out his name again as I felt my climax building up in me. I bucked up one more time, my legs pinning him into me, and at the same moment, with one final stroke, I felt his release. His whole body tensed over me as I pulsed around him, his name my only litany.

Liam collapsed next to me, his lips at my ear. "Are you okay?"

I smiled, unable to speak yet as my heart still raced. "So much better than okay. So much better."

He pulled me with him to lie on my side so that he stayed within me. I slid my arms around and held him close, the thud of his heartbeat a perfect lullaby to lure me to sleep.

Ch♥pter Fifteen

"**W**HERE'S THE BAG with the gift in it?" I stood next to Liam's car, poking into the trunk. "Did you bring it down?"

"It's in the backseat." Liam came up next to me, carrying a garment bag. "I figured it was safer there from being broken."

"Good thinking." I wrapped my arms around him from the back and tip-toed up to kiss his neck. "Must be why I have you around."

"Well, it's one reason." He caught my hand and lifted it to his lips to kiss my fingers. "I think that's it. Are you ready to go?"

"Yup." We climbed into the car, and Liam pulled away from the curb. I sent my mom a quick text to tell her we were on our way.

"I hope you're ready for this." I put away my phone and glanced at Liam.

"What? I've already met your family. What's the big deal?"

I shook my head. "Oh, sweetie, you met some of my

family. And believe me, if you've never been to an Italian wedding, you have no idea what you're in for. It's going to be wild."

"I can do wild."

"Yeah, you keep thinking that."

He smirked. "Baby, we could stop on the way, and I can show you how well I do wild."

I sighed. "Don't tempt me. Bad enough I'm worried that my mom's going to take one look at me and know I'm having sex."

Liam's eyebrows rose. "Is that her superpower? She can tell when people are having sex?"

"I don't think it extends to the general population. Probably just her children." I giggled. "I remember the night of Carl's prom. He and Angela sealed the deal that night, but of course no one knew. Except Ma. He walked in the door, and she smacked him in the back of the head and told him he was an idiot. Then she cried, and she told him she hoped he'd taken care of Ange." I shook my head, remembering.

"So what do I have to expect from this wedding? Now you have me worried."

"Oh, nothing to be concerned about. It'll be fun. There'll be more food than we can eat, and everyone will be drinking grappa and limoncello. And the dancing ...well, you've never seen dancing until you've been to a big Italian wedding. All my uncles will ask you when you're going to do the right thing by me, and my aunts will pinch your cheek and tell you how cute you are. Oh, and if anyone asks if you're Catholic, say yes."

"But I'm not."

"I know, but no one's going to remember anyway, and it will just be easier."

We turned on some Frank, and I sang along to make

Liam smile as we drove. As I watched the pines flying past us out the window, I thought that I was happier than I could remember. Coming home with my boyfriend for a big family wedding was exciting. I'd been thrilled for Carl and Angela anyway, but being able to share the day with Liam was going to make it even better.

"What are you doing?" Liam smiled at me as we turned down the street where my parents lived.

"Hmm? Oh." I looked down at my hand and realized I'd been leaning on the dash, almost trying to push the car faster. "I guess I'm anxious to get there. Ma's a nervous wreck about the rehearsal dinner being at Cucina Felice, I want to help her if I can."

"Do you know, the cadence of your speech changes the closer you get to home? Also whenever you talk to your mother on the phone. It's crazy."

I grinned. "You can take the Italian girl out of the neighborhood, but you can't take the neighborhood out of her."

We carried our bags into the house. It was a bedlam of activity, with my grandparents and two aunts in the kitchen, while my uncles and cousins sat around in the living room.

"Ava Catarine!" My Nonna greeted me with outstretched arms. "Look at you, so pretty, so grown up! Look at her, Nancy."

"I see her, Ma. Good you're here, Ava. We need all the hands we can get. Your mother's on the edge of a breakdown. I sent her to rest with a cup of tea—and I'm not ashamed to say I put a little something extra in there for her."

"Okay, I'll drop my bag and dive in." I paused, glancing back at Liam, who was standing in the middle of the room, our suitcases in his hands. "Oh—everybody!"

I shouted, using my family voice, the one that carried through at least three rooms. Everyone turned to me as conversation stopped.

"This is Liam Bailey. He's my boyfriend, and he came down for the wedding with me. Be nice to him, and don't ask him any questions. Introduce yourselves."

There was a moment of silence and then the talking started up again. My cousin stood up to help Liam with the suitcases, and they went upstairs.

"He's cute, Ava." Aunt Leonora patted my arm. "Here, put on this apron so you keep your dress nice. Cut up those onions, will you—we're putting the salads together at the restaurant, but we're chopping here, to stay out of the way, since they're doing most of the cooking there."

Liam came back downstairs. After being shuffled from one group to another, meeting more people than he'd ever remember, he ended up at the kitchen table next to Nonna.

"Mary Adela, get me the scalabage!" Aunt Leonora stood by the sink, a huge steaming pot in her hands. "This damn macaroni is heavy."

My cousin came running with the colander. She tossed it in the sink, and Aunt Leonora poured the pasta into it.

"What's a scalabage?" Liam leaned to whisper to me.

I smiled. "It's slang Italian for pasta strainer. Most of us, especially the older ones, speak English with a lot of Italian words thrown in. Some of them are legit, some of kind of evolved over the years."

"It takes a while before you'll understand us all." Nonna patted his arm. "That's okay, you don't get something, you ask me. Now how long you been with my granddaughter Ava?"

"Nonna, no third degree." I dropped another section of onion into the bowl.

"What?" She spread her hands out, innocent. "I can't talk now?"

"No, of course you can, but—"

"Ava! When did you get here? Why didn't anyone tell me she was here? I was up there worried to death she'd gone off the road, God forbid." My mother appeared in the doorway of the kitchen, wearing her robe, with her hair up in curlers and strain on her face.

"I'm sorry, Ma, I got here and they put me right to work."

"Did you sleep, Frannie?" Aunt Nancy looked up from the red gravy she was stirring.

"I did, thank you. Liam, so good to see you again!" She crossed the kitchen to hug him and pat me on the shoulder. "It's time to get ready for church. I told your father we'd just meet him there, that I could ride with you two."

"Okay, we'll go get dressed." I stood up and kissed my mother's cheek. "It's all going to be wonderful, Ma. Don't worry."

She smiled, and then she looked at me with narrowed eyes. Blood rushed to my face, and I dropped my gaze. She wouldn't say anything here, in front of the family, but she knew.

Then Liam stood next to me and rested a hand on my shoulder. "Is there anything I can do to help, Mrs. DiMartino?"

My mother's face softened, and she glanced from Liam to me.

"You're a good boy. No, just go on, get ready for the church."

199

THE REHEARSAL WAS a mess. Half of Angela's bridesmaids were her cousins, and they got stuck in traffic on the way to the church. The organist had all the wrong music, and the priest, who was new to our parish, kept calling my brother Chris instead of Carl.

But it didn't matter at all to my brother and his fiancée. I watched them together, and I saw the way his eyes softened when she came down the aisle. As they practiced their vows, I glanced to the back of the church where Liam sat. Our eyes met and held.

After an hour and a half, my brother announced that they'd had enough practice. It was now time to eat. Everyone drove to Cucina Felice, which was open that night only for the families.

And my family had done a wonderful job. There was candlelight everywhere, and tulle draped over the windows and doorways. Food and drink were plenteous. My parents moved around the room, gracious hosts seeing to their guests' comfort. I was proud of them. I was proud of all of us.

Frankie came skipping up to me for a hug. "Auntie Ave, wait 'til you see my dress for tomorrow! Auntie Ange says I'm gonna be a princess."

I touched her black curls. "I can't wait, sweetie."

She laughed and climbed into a chair near me, breaking off a hunk of bread like the seasoned pro she was. She leaned one small hand on Liam's knee and whispered into his ear. He grinned and pulled her onto his lap, where she sat in contentment, munching away. It gave me a brandnew kind of thrill, watching him as he slid one large tanned hand over her curls.

As the evening wore down, my mother came over and slipped an arm around Liam's shoulder. "Liam, would you do me a huge favor? My parents are staying at my sister's house, but Nancy went home early with a headache. Could you drive them over?"

"Of course, we can do that." Liam stood, pulled out his keys, and offered me his hand.

"Actually, I was hoping Ava could stay to help me with a few things here, if that's okay."

Panic gripped me. This was it. This was when she was going to tell me she knew what I'd done and remind me what a mistake that could be. I looked up at Liam, and though I knew he read the terror in my eyes, he only smiled.

"Sure." He bent to kiss my cheek and whisper in my ear.

"Have fun."

With everyone pitching in, clean up didn't take long. My mother and I were leaving the restaurant, heading home, before I knew it.

"I thought Daddy was coming with us." I climbed in as my mother turned the ignition.

"He's riding home with your brothers. I wanted to have this time with just us."

My heart flipped over. "Oh." I struggled for something to say, anything to keep her from talking about Liam and me. "I'm sorry the rehearsal was such a disaster."

"Not me! Bad rehearsal, good wedding. Trust me, it never fails."

She backed out of the parking lot and turned onto the road. "I'm happy for your brother. I love Angela like she's one of my own. She practically is, as long as she and Carl have been a couple. This is a happy day. Tomorrow will be even better. But you know ..." Her voice trailed off, and a sob caught in her throat. "Every happy day from now until forever will always have some sadness, because our Antonia should be here with us."

Tears blinded me, and I put my fist to my mouth. My sister had been on my mind all day: she should have been cutting onions with me at the table, making faces at the rehearsal, fussing over her daughter's dress for tomorrow. But she wasn't. All the places she should have been were empty.

"I miss her every day." My mother dashed at the tears running down her face. "Every day, I talk to her while I'm getting up, getting ready. When I go over to open the restaurant. When I drop Frankie at pre-school. But it's worse on days like this, when everyone's together."

"I miss her too, Ma." I sniffed. "So much."

"I know you do. That's why I wanted this time with you. My sisters, my mother, of course your father and the boys, they miss her. But not like us. And I needed to just be with you, and cry a little. Remember."

I reached across the seat and gripped my mother's hand. "Wouldn't she have loved all the family together today?"

"She would have. But I'll tell you something, she would have hated those pink dresses Angela picked out for all of you. Can you just hear her now?"

And so we drove home, laughing through our tears, remembering, and somehow it brought Antonia closer to us again. I could almost hear her giggle and smell her perfume.

When I climbed out of the car, still wiping away tears, my mother gripped me and pulled me to her for a hug.

"I'm proud of you, Ava. Proud of your hard work and what you're doing." She stood back and patted my cheek.

"Don't think I don't know things are hot and heavy with you and Liam. I don't like it ...but I like him. And I understand. I remember what it was like to be young. It makes me lighter to know you have someone who loves you like that."

"Ma, it's not like that. Not yet. It's new." I glanced up to the light in my bedroom, where Liam was probably getting ready for bed.

"Don't tell me what I don't know. He looks at you with love. When you know, you know." She took my hand. "All right now, let's go in, and watch your father and the boys pretend they don't see our wet faces. Because don't think they weren't doing the same thing all the way home."

MY MOTHER'S PREDICTION for the wedding turned out to be on target. The ceremony was absolutely perfect, beautiful from beginning to end. I stood at the front of the church in my long pink dress, tears streaming down my face as I listened to my big brother pledge his undying devotion to Angela.

"You look gorgeous." Liam met me in the narthex and kissed me, quickly and discreetly. "Are you okay? I saw you crying."

"Weddings always make me cry." I smiled. "I'm fine. We're doing pictures next. Do you want to come with us, or go ahead to the reception?"

One side of mouth lifted. "I think I'll stick with you, if it's okay. I'm kind of afraid to be around the family without you to protect me."

Within about an hour, we were at the reception. Angela's parents had rented a beautiful hall that used to be a theatre, and it was everything I knew Angela had wanted. I laughed when we all danced into the room as we were announced and took our places at the head table. Angela had kindly seated Liam next to me at the main table, so we were able to eat together.

"I thought you were exaggerating about the food!" He held his stomach. "Every course is better than the last!"

We had started with soup, then salad, a pasta course ...and then the main entrée, chicken or steak. Desserts was yet to be served, and I couldn't even think about it.

"Told you so." I pointed to the empty shot glass next to his place. "What's that?"

Liam grimaced. "One of your uncles gave it to me. Told me all Italians had to drink grappa at a wedding. He had a shot, too, but he didn't drink his when I did mine. I asked him why, and he said it was horrible stuff he'd never touch."

We both laughed. "You should try the limoncello, though. It's really good. My uncle John bottles his own, and that's what they're serving tonight."

When the dancing began, I had to do one go-round with the groomsman who was my partner for the traditional wedding party dance. And then the music changed.

"What's this?" Liam had to shout to be heard over the music and the roar of approval from the entire crowd.

"It's the Tarantella!" I grabbed his hand. "Come on. It's the traditional Italian wedding dance. Everyone has to do it."

We joined the circle, going around and then linking elbows to spin our partners. I laughed so hard my sides ached. Liam pulled me close to him and kissed me hard.

"Is that the grappa?" I touched his face, looking up into those intoxicating blue eyes.

"No, that's you, making me drunk just watching you laugh and dance. I love seeing you like this. No worrying, no over thinking everything ...just perfect."

I slid my hand into his, smiling into his eyes. "Are you brave enough to come meet some more family? There are a few people I should say hello to."

He squeezed my hand. "Sure. Lead the way."

We made the rounds, visiting tables of friends and family. I introduced Liam, getting a little thrill each time I got to say the words 'my boyfriend'.

After the bouquet toss, the garter throw, the money dance and the cake cutting, everything slowed down. When I heard the strains of one of my favorite Sinatra songs, I smiled up at Liam at the same time that he looked down.

"Dance with me?" He held out his hand.

We moved onto the dance floor, our bodies pressed tight as Frank and his daughter Nancy sang about saying something stupid.

"Would it be stupid?" Liam whispered in my ear, sending shivers down my spine.

"Would what be stupid?"

"If I said it. If I said ...I love you."

I held my breath, leaning my ear against his chest. His arms tightened around me.

"It would only be stupid if you didn't mean it." I tilted my head up a little so that he could hear me.

"And if I do?"

"Then ...I guess it would be stupid not to say it."

His fingers came down to caress my chin, lift my eyes to his. "I love you, Ava."

I caught my lip between my teeth and smiled, letting every bit of yearning and love flow through me. "I love you, Liam."

He leaned over, covering my mouth with a kiss that was full of every promise I'd ever wanted.

Ch♥pter Sixteen

MY PARENTS HOSTED a post-wedding buffet breakfast at the restaurant on Sunday. Liam and I stayed until about noon.

"Be careful driving back." My mother hugged Liam. "And text me the minute you get there." She kissed my cheek.

"Don't forget. You know how your mother worries." My father wrapped me in a bear hug and shook Liam's hand.

"I will. I promise. It was all so beautiful, Ma, Daddy. Thank you for making this weekend so wonderful for Carl and Ange. For all of us."

My mother dabbed at her eyes, and my father cleared his throat. "Family is everything. You know that. These days ...they're good days. Days when we get to celebrate. They're what get us through the not-so-good days." He pulled my mother toward him in a side hug.

Liam helped me into the car and gave my parents one last wave as we drove away.

"That's what I want." He grabbed at my hand. "This

weekend ...it was real. I've been to lots of weddings. Big fancy ones. And none of them felt real like Carl and Angela's did."

I held tight to his hand. "I know. I forget sometimes. . you know, being away. The family seems like a burden. Like something I don't need. Then a weekend like this happens, and I remember it all. I know why it's important. All of them, my grandparents, my aunts and uncle and cousins, my parents ...they made me who I am."

A buzzing sounded, and Liam reached into his back pocket. He tossed me his phone. "Can you check on that?"

I looked at the screen. "It's your father."

Liam scowled. "Hit ignore, please."

"Are you sure? You don't want to talk to him?"

"I'm sure."

I hit the button and handed it back to him.

"Liam, this thing with your parents ...you've got to figure it out."

His mouth tightened. "Not much to figure out. As long as I do what my father wants, he's happy. If I don't ..." He shrugged. "He always gets his way."

"But you don't know that. If you just talk to him, tell him that you don't want to go into politics, maybe he'll listen."

"I've been saying it one way or another for a while now. He thinks he knows what's best."

I stared out my window. "Liam, I'd like to meet them. I think I should."

"No. Absolutely not."

I swallowed. "Why? Are you ashamed of me?"

"Hell, no. Never. I'm ashamed of them."

"But we're part of each other's lives now, Liam. That's the good, the bad and ugly. You met my whole family. Shouldn't I at least meet your parents?"

He gripped the steering wheel. "Ava, you are the one good and pure thing in my life. You're the real. I don't want to fuck that up by letting my parents torture you."

I drew in a deep breath. "Am I temporary?"

"What? No, of course not. Why would you ask that?"

"Because if you expect me to be part of your life for any length of time, I'm going to have to have interaction with your family."

"Not if I don't."

I screwed together my forehead. "What's that supposed to mean?"

"Maybe I won't see my parents again. Maybe ...I make my own decisions and I live my own life, and I just cut them out."

My mouth opened in shock. "How on earth can you even consider that? Liam, they might be screwed up, but they're your mother and father."

"Ava, I told you. They're not like your parents. You have no idea." He shot me a glance. "I don't want to talk about them anymore. Just leave it alone."

AND I DID. For a solid week, I didn't mention Liam's parents or suggest that he reach out to them. We settled into our normal routine of classes, track meets and hours spent just being with each other. Finals were underway, and I was stressed, trying to balance my new life with studying, homework and internship applications. Liam had decided to stay at Birch for the summer, and I desperately wanted to do the same.

The day I took my Behavior Disorders final, I met Liam for a run after the test. I still wasn't hooked on running, but I was hooked on Liam ...particularly in his running shorts and tight shirts. That was all the inspiration I needed. It even made up for the pain of putting on the running bra, since Liam was always happy to help me take it off.

We went a little longer, ran a little harder that day. Liam spent the last leg of the run telling me what he liked about my boobs.

"I like it when you wear a low-cut top, and you bend over to get something. And I like it when you've just gotten up in the morning, and you're not wearing a bra under your t-shirt, and your nipples pucker against the cloth. And I like when we're making love, and I just touch my mouth to the tip, and you go crazy."

I stopped, leaning over, panting. "Speaking of being crazy. Are you doing this on purpose? To make me run faster?"

"No." He grabbed my hand and pulled me close. "I'm just giving you helpful information. But now that you mention it, we're right here by my room. I think we've run long enough."

When we got back to his room, we were on fire for each other; we didn't wait to open the door before he shoved me up against it, grinding his erection against me as I wrapped my legs around his waist. His hand was on my breast, pinching hard at my nipple through the running bra.

"Open the door." I growled it against his lips.

"Trying." He groped blindly for the doorknob, and when he finally turned it, we half-fell into the room, laughing.

I saw him first. A man sat in the room on Liam's wooden desk chair. He was older and well-dressed, and above his pristine, perfectly-pressed collar, he wore an expression of surprise and distaste.

Shit.

I struggled to get down, and Liam, still not seeing, grabbed my ass. "Where do you think you're going? I'm going to take you up against that wall, right now." He finally saw my face and turned to follow the direction of my stare.

Liam lowered me slowly to the ground and moved to stand between his father and me. He glanced at him and then spoke without any expression in his voice.

"Dad. What are you doing here?"

"Well, Liam, considering that you haven't taken any of our telephone calls or returned any messages in over a month, your mother and I were concerned about you." Mr. Bailey's eyes flickered over me. "I can see you're well. Maybe you should have had some consideration for your mother. She worries."

I closed my eyes, remembering just a few weeks ago when we were leaving my parents' house, my father saying almost those same words.

Don't forget to text your mother when you get home. You know how she worries.

But what Liam's father just said didn't have any truth or emotion behind it. It was just another way to make his son feel guilty, to manipulate him. I closed my hands around Liam's arm and leaned into his back. If I couldn't do anything else in this situation, I could at least remind him that he wasn't alone.

"I've been ... busy." Liam's voice was still neutral. "And frankly, I didn't have anything to say to either of you."

His father raised one eyebrow.

"I don't know what that's supposed mean. Did something happen that I'm not aware of, son? Did your mother

211

and I commit some sort of parental faux pas that you're punishing us for? Because all I can remember is that we've raised you with every advantage and given you every opportunity." He let his eyes wander past his son to rake over me. "Something's been different about you the past few months. I thought maybe it was just a phase, just growing pains that all children go through, but now I'm beginning to wonder if it might be the company you've been keeping."

Ah. That was me. *The company he was keeping.* I tried to keep my breathing even and remember that this man didn't know me. He had no idea that Liam and I were dating, because Liam had never told his parents about me; to him, I was just the girl who came into the room with her legs wrapped around his son. I had to admit that my own parents wouldn't be very understanding under those circumstances either.

Liam's hand, resting against mine, flinched. I felt him take a deep breath. "Sorry, I'm being rude. Dad, this is Ava DiMartino. My girlfriend. Ava, babe, this is my father. The senator." I couldn't see Liam's face, but I felt his body stiffen as he continued to speak. "My father, who has given me every opportunity and advantage growing up, as long as they were the ones that he felt were worthwhile."

I peeked out from behind his back, though I could feel that he didn't want me moving any closer. I cleared my throat.

"It's nice to meet you, Senator Bailey. Liam has told me so much about you."

His lips stretched into a parody of a smile. "I wish I could say the same. My son has neglected to mention much about his life lately." The tone in his voice implied that perhaps in me, he'd found the reason for that lacking. I stiffened my spine.

"Why should I talk, Dad, when no one's listening?" Liam was calm, but I recognized it as the quiet that meant he was incredibly angry and barely holding onto control.

The senator sighed and shook his head. "Liam, you have this imagined sense of neglect. I want you to remember how often your mother and I have made the trip down here to see you at school. The track meets we've attended. You are and have always been our chief priority. And I'm here today to let you know that I was able to pull some strings, work my magic, and I got you that internship in Washington. The one you were supposed to apply for two months ago. So I'd like you to tell me, when have I not listened to you, son?"

"How about every single time I've told you I don't think I want a life in politics? Every time I said I'd like to explore my other options. Every time I mentioned the idea of doing something other than what you've chosen for me to do? And this. Now. I don't want the fucking internship in Washington. I didn't apply because I have no intention of going down there. So you can un-pull your strings and work your magic again to get me out of it."

Senator Bailey shifted in the chair, and I heard it creak. "Liam, this is neither the time nor the place. We don't air our misunderstandings in front of strangers."

Liam took one step forward, his hands clenched at his sides. "First of all, Dad, this is not a misunderstanding. Unless you're saying you don't remember me telling you that I didn't want the gig in DC. Unless you mean you misunderstood me when I told you the last time you and Mother were here that there was no way in hell I was taking it.

"And second, Ava is not a stranger. There's nothing you can't say in front of her, because I share everything with her. She already knows how screwed up our family is."

The senator's mouth tightened into a thin, hard line. "Watch your mouth, son. I don't expect to be spoken to like that. Keep in mind that I'm still your father, even if you're going through some kind of delayed teen-age rebellion."

Liam ran his hand through his hair, still damp from our run. "I'm not a teen-ager, Dad. And this isn't rebellion, it's me taking charge of my own life, finally. About time, don't you think? Oh, and don't worry, Dad. I never forget who my father is." He dropped his voice until it was dangerously low and hard. "He's a fucking hypocrite."

His father shot to his feet. "That's enough, Liam. You can stand there and throw accusations at me for whatever imagined offenses I've committed—"

"No, Dad, it wasn't an imagined offense. I didn't imagine the woman you were fucking in my mother's bed last December."

The senator's face went from red to pale, and I caught the twitch in his left eye. "Liam, that is enough." His angry stare shifted to me momentarily before returning to his son.

"I told you, Dad, you can say anything you want in front of Ava. She knows everything. So why don't you try to make sense of the whole thing to me again? I'm sure we'd all like to hear that explanation. I'm wonder if Mother might be interested, too. When she asks you why I don't call or come home anymore, do you tell her it's because I never know what I'm going to find?"

I ventured to step out behind Liam. "Why don't we all take a minute to cool off before someone says something he doesn't mean?"

Liam grasped my arm and shoved me behind him again. "Stay out of this, Ava. Don't worry, I mean everything I say. Every fucking word."

"Maybe this girl has a point, Liam. I'll step out now, let you get a shower, think about what you're saying here. What it is you really want. Then I'll take you out to dinner, just the two of us. We'll work this out. What we're talking about isn't an issue to be discussed in front of someone who ...may be putting the wrong kind of pressure on you."

"*This girl,* Dad, is Ava. She's the kind of person who makes me want to be better than I am, to be my best. She makes me happy, just by being around her." He leaned forward and lowered his voice. "You might like to know that *this girl* is at the top of our class academically. She works harder than anyone I know. And believe it or not, she's the one who's been trying to get me to talk to you for the last few weeks. Because she can't imagine a family where the parents and children don't get along. So before you go laying the blame on *this girl*, you should stop and think about what you want our relationship to be in the future. Whether you expect to have any contact with me at all. Because *this girl* isn't going anywhere."

The senator's frosty glare landed on me before returning to his son. "You know, son, I'm trying to give you some latitude here, because it's real easy to talk about hypocrisy and ideals from the vantage point of twenty-one years old. I'm human, Liam. When I was your age, I liked to have my fun, too. I sowed my share of wild oats with girls who weren't ...long-term material." This time, his eyes stayed on me as he continued. "I'm happy that I listened to my own father's advice. The same words I passed down to you. There are girls you marry. Nice girls, from good families, who know how to act in public, girls who will give you connections and never embarrass you. And then there are the girls you fuck. Those are the ones who give you a good time, but they can't give you anything else. They're the ones you leave behind."

I couldn't breathe. It felt a little like the night I'd drunk too much jungle juice at Jeff's house; the room tilted, and I grabbed at the door to stay upright.

"This new friends of yours ...whatever your name is, dear ...I think we all know into which category she falls."

That was it. I took a step backwards, out through the open door. "I ...I have to go. I'm sorry, Liam. I can't stay here anymore."

Tears blinded me as I wheeled out of the room and into the hallway. I had to get out of there, out of the building, away from both of them.

"Ava!" Liam's voice rang out, following me down the hallway. "Ava, wait. Don't leave. I'll make him go. Just don't leave."

I didn't turn around, and I didn't stop until I was back in my own dorm. I pushed past the crowds, desperate to get to the sanctity of my own room. A few of the freshman girls called my name, tried to get my attention, but for the first time ever, I ignored them and walked away.

Julia was sitting in her desk when I burst through the door. She looked up at me, startled.

"Hey, I thought you were staying with Liam ..." Her voice trailed off, as her eyes took me in. "Oh, sweetie. Ava, what happened? What's wrong?"

I threw myself across my bed, buried my face in my pillow and cried.

Ch♥pter Seventeen

I DON'T KNOW how long I sobbed as Julia sat on the bed next to me. She pulled me into her arms, and we lay there as I poured out the whole ugly conversation.

"He said ...he said I was a girl to fuck. A girl who gets left behind, because she's not good enough for anything else." I wiped my face, taking a deep breath against Julia's shoulder. "And I couldn't say anything, because I *am* fucking his son. For God's sake, Jules, we were practically doing it when we walked into the room. I was wrapped around his waist, and his hand was ..." I closed my eyes.

Julia sighed. "Liam's making this a habit, walking into rooms with his hand down a girl's shirt and getting a surprise." When I began to sob harder, she shook her head. "I'm sorry. Too soon. Oh, Ave, I'm so sorry about this whole thing. But you can't really believe that's what Liam thinks about you."

I balled up my pillow and leaned my chin against it. "I don't know what to think. Liam might not be feeling that way right now, but what's going to happen later? I don't want to be the one he leaves behind, but I also don't want to be the one who hurts his career. Ruins his life. And what if he only keeps me around because he feels sorry for me? Or to get back at his dad? Damn it, Jules, what if this whole thing with me is just Liam's way to screw his father, to throw it in his face after what he found out?"

"You don't seriously think that's true. Come on, Ava. What happened to the girl who spent weeks trying to convince me that Liam Bailey wasn't a dick? That he's not out to hurt you?"

"I don't think he'd do it on purpose. He probably doesn't even realize that he's dating me to get back at his father."

"That sounds like some kind of psych crap you heard in a class. Stop and think about what you're saying."

"I am. God, Jules, maybe I was just as much of an idiot as I thought back in the beginning. Why the hell would Liam Bailey be interested in someone like me? I don't do country clubs or tennis. I don't have family money. I come from immigrants. Yeah, they're good people, hard-working, but they're not the kind of people the Baileys would want marrying into their precious family."

"Ava, stop it. This isn't the Middle Ages. Or even the fifties. That kind of thinking is bullshit. People marry who they want to marry."

"You didn't hear Liam's father talking. It might not be that clear cut, but I for sure don't fall into the category of girls he wants for his son." I took a deep breath and pushed to sit up. "I can't do it, Julia. No matter what Liam says, I'll always be second-guessing it. Second-guessing *us*. Knowing that people are going to be looking at us together, thinking to themselves, *what's Liam Bailey doing with someone like her?* I can't live like that."

"God, Ava, you're getting way ahead of yourself. No

one's talking about marriage except Liam's father, who is clearly a dickwad. You don't have to make this decision right now. Just keep things like they are, and when the time comes, you can worry about all this."

I shook my head. "I'm not like that, Jules. I know I'm not ready to get married, but I can't be with Liam if I'm not good enough for him."

"Not good enough? Are you crazy? You're *too* good for him. I've been saying that all along." Her firm voice, ringing with her confidence in me, made cry all over again. She pulled me back into a hug.

"Oh, sweetie, don't. Please." She stroked my hair. "Listen to me, Ave. You know I haven't been the biggest Liam Bailey fan ...like, ever. I was the one who tried to talk you out of him at every turn, right? I was sure he was playing you, or he was going to end up breaking your heart. But all along, you've told me that there's something in this boy that's worthwhile. Something special, something only you could see. And the last few weeks, I can see it. His eyes, when you walk into the room ...they never leave you. He's not that stiff, closed-off jerk I dated for much too long. With you, he opens up, and he seems ..." She tilted her head, thinking. "I don't know. Content, maybe."

I sniffled. "You're just saying that to make me feel better."

"No, I absolutely am not. I wouldn't. If this had happened a month ago, I would have been the one doing the I-told-you-so dance all over you. But I'd be wrong."

I shook my head, but I couldn't manage any words.

"And Ava ...you've changed, too. I love you, and I always have and I always will. But up until this year, you were closed-off. I knew you were always in my corner, and you'd do anything for me, but there was this part of you that you kept away. You were so focused and driven that sometimes it scared me. Liam's changed that in you. You smile all the time now. You laugh. You're ...softer."

Another sob rattled from my chest. "There's a reason hard things last longer. Soft things get hurt. They don't have endurance. And they get left behind."

"That's not true. You have endurance. I would never leave you behind. And neither would Liam."

Mention of his name just made me cry again, and finally Julia gave up on logic. She just held me while I wept until my sobs turned to hiccups. Once I'd settled down into sniffles, she went to the student union to get us soup for dinner. I didn't think I could keep anything else down.

Alone, I tried to push away all thoughts of Liam and his father. I picked up my Cognition textbook, but it caught on my rosary, tipping over the frame with Antonia's photo.

I drew in a shuddering breath and set the picture upright. I wished I could call my sister right now, ask her what to do. She would've liked Liam, I thought, at least once she'd gotten to know him. She probably would've kicked his ass for letting his dad talk like that. Not that he had, not really; he'd defended me up to the minute I ran away. I was fairly sure Antonia would've told me not to give up on love, even when it hurt. Thinking about her and what she might have said made me cry all over again.

I had turned off my phone, not wanting to see Liam's texts or calls. But I'd expected he would come over, try to see me. When the hours went on, and nothing happened, a sense of dread filled me. He wasn't coming. His father had convinced him that I wasn't worth his time. He'd finally realized that he didn't love me. I was just an aberration—what had I told him this past winter? *Temporary insanity.*

My last exam was the next morning, but I didn't even

bother opening a book. I knew nothing I read would stick at this point. I had a good grasp of the material, and right now, I didn't care anyway. Pass, fail, get kicked out of school ...what did it matter?

The next morning, I was hung over. My stomach was in knots, my throat hurt and my body ached. I stayed in bed until the last possible minute, and then pulled on my yoga pants and an old t-shirt. Even that simple act made me cry, remembering Liam making fun of me for wearing the pants without going to the class.

I slid into my classroom just as the exams were distributed. For two blessed hours, I didn't have to time to think about anything but Cognition. It was just the paper, my pencil and me. The rest of the world ceased to exist.

When the test was over, I walked back to the dorm in a daze. I only wanted my bed, the quiet and the dark. Just a little peace.

Julia was putting clothes into a bag when I opened the door. She looked up at me and smiled.

"How did it go?"

I shrugged. "I think I did okay. It's over." I fell into my bed. "It's all over. The last exam of junior year."

She grinned. "I know. I'm pretty sure I kicked ass on my history of journalism final. So I'm going over to Jesse's to celebrate." She paused, glancing at me. "Will you be okay? Do you want to come with me?"

I shook my head. "No. God, no. No offense, Jules, but being around you and Jesse right now is so not what I need. I just want to lay here in my bed and die."

"No dying. You've still got the fun of checking all the freshmen out of their dorms tomorrow and the next day. You wouldn't want to miss that. And at least three girls have come by looking for you. They all have questions. Lucky you."

I groaned. "Put a pillow over my head. It's a mercy killing. I'll write a note."

"Don't even joke about that." She sat down on the edge of my bed. "Seriously, will you be okay? I'll stay if you need me. Jesse can wait."

I squeezed her hand. "Thanks, Jules. But no. I really just want to be alone. I promise I won't do anything desperate. But I just want to crawl into bed and sleep for about a week. And then I'll see what the world feels like after that."

"Okay." She leaned over to hug me from behind. "Love you, Ave. Call me if you need anything."

She left, swinging her bag over her arm, and I turned my face into the depths of my pillow. I heard her voice in the hall, probably talking to some freshman girl. Hopefully telling said girl that I was horribly sick and to leave me alone.

The door opened again. Without moving, I groaned. "For the love of everything holy, tell them to go away. I don't want to see anyone. Or talk to anyone."

The door closed with a click, and a moment later, the bed sagged next to me.

"Sorry, you don't get a choice in this."

My heart skipped. *Liam*. I could feel his warmth next to my hip, smell his scent. But I didn't move. I didn't even breathe.

"Ava ...turn over. Come on. Talk to me."

I shook my head against the pillow. "Go away, Liam. I can't deal with this."

"Then deal with me. I want to see your eyes. I need to see that beautiful face."

I snorted. "You're out of luck. This face is red and ugly from crying for almost twenty-four hours straight. Trust me, it's not what you want to see."

He took hold of my shoulder and pushed until I was on my back. He traced the edge of my cheek with one finger.

"I will always want to see this face. No matter what. This face is gorgeous all the time. And it's the face I love."

Tears I thought had dried up brimmed in my eyes. "No, it's the face of a girl you leave behind. A girl who's only good enough to ..." I couldn't say the words.

"Ava, my father is a fucking idiot. And I told him that. I told him I wasn't taking his internship. I was going to make it a surprise for you, but I got a job this summer in the history department, here. I'm going to stay at Birch all summer. With you."

I shook my head. "I'm not getting in the middle of you and your parents. I won't be the reason you can't have a relationship with them."

Liam sighed. "You're not. I talked to my dad for a long time last night. That's why I didn't come over here. By the time he finally left, it was late and I knew we both had finals this morning. I didn't want to screw up your test."

I sniffed. "You wouldn't have. I don't care about it, anyway. You're more important."

He leaned down and pulled me to sit, gathering me into his arms. "That's what I told my father. You, Ava Catarine DiMartino, are not a girl who gets left behind. You never were, and you never will be. You're the girl I love. The girl I want with me always."

I let my head fall onto his shoulder. "The things he said, Liam ...they were horrible. I keep hearing him."

His arms tightened around me. "I know. I told him that if he ever spoke that way to you or in front of you again, it would be the last time he ever saw me. I think he got the message." He ran his hand down my hair, cupped

223

my face. "Ava, I don't know if he's ever going to change. But the important thing is that I stood up to him. I showed him that I'll fight for what's important to me. Including choosing my own future, making my own plans. And you. You are the most important plan, the one crucial element. Without you, the rest of it doesn't make sense."

I swallowed back a shuddering sob. "I don't want to be your rebellion against your parents. I need to know that you love me for who I am, not just because I piss off your mom and dad."

He laughed, burying his face in my hair. "Baby, that's just an added benefit. I love you because you're who you are. You make me better. When I'm around you, you make me feel ...peaceful. And then I kiss you ..." He brought his mouth down to cover mine in one searing, passionate sweep. "And peace explodes into this powerful need."

I gripped his shoulders, holding him close. "I need you, too. When you touch me, everything stops. Nothing exists but you, and me, and your hands on me. Your lips."

I rose on my knees and then straddled him, bringing my mouth up for a kiss that wiped every other thought from my mind. And then I sat back and stared into his blue eyes.

"So we can't live without each other. Is that a good enough reason to possibly alienate your parents?"

He dropped his forehead onto my shoulder. "Trust me. They won't stay alienated. Especially my mother—she'll be calling this week, wanting to meet you out of curiosity if nothing else. No, it was time to make this stand. It's all going to work out. But you've got to promise me that you won't bail if things get rough again. And they're going to. You've got to trust me, and stick with me. Don't run away."

"I'll do my best. I won't run unless you're with me."

He smiled into my eyes. "Last night, when I couldn't sleep, worried I'd lost you, I put on your play list. And *All The Way* came on. I started thinking ...that's how I want to love you. Like it says—come what may. Can you trust me to do that?"

I nuzzled his neck. "I'm keeping you, Liam. I probably don't deserve you, but I'm keeping you anyway."

He smiled against my lips. "You deserve so much more. Infinitely more. But I promise, I'm going to be the person who makes you happy. You won't regret keeping me. I love you, Ava. I love you all the way."

I closed my eyes as he kissed down my neck. "I love you, Liam."

The sun filled my room, and in the hallways, I could hear freshmen having end-of-the-year tantrums. The world was spinning around us, but within the cocoon of Liam's arms, I was safe, and quiet, and content.

Epil♥gue

"**H**EY, LIAM, BRING out the ice cream, will you? If you're not too busy groping Ava, that is."

Giff's voice floated in from outside, and I giggled, hiding my face in the crook of Liam's neck. He had me on the counter, and he stood between my knees, his arms wrapped around me, his hand up my shirt and his mouth on my breast.

"Fucking Giff." His words were muffled and just made me laugh more.

People were just beginning to arrive for our impromptu housewarming dessert party. It had been nearly a month since Liam and I had moved into the townhouse a block down from where Jeff and Giff lived. It was Jeff who had told us that one of his neighbors needed a last-minute tenant, giving us the opportunity to rent the house for the next year.

Moving in together had been a natural conclusion; we were always at each other's room, and both of our roommates made it an easy decision. Giff had been staying with Jeff anyway, and Julia was practically living with Jesse. I was pretty sure she'd end the summer with a ring on her finger.

Liam was working at the history department at Birch, and he loved it. He was talking about maybe getting his masters degree and teaching after graduation. His parents still weren't happy with this decision, but they had thawed enough to come down and take us both out to dinner. While the senator still couldn't look me in the eye, his wife had been pleasant. I was hopeful that they might come to accept me. Someday.

I was busy with the internship I'd gotten with a local ad agency. It was so much fun to use the psychology I'd been learning; since the company was so small, they often let me contribute ideas to some of their campaigns. Most of the time, though, I was filing papers and answering phones. It was a start.

My parents had reluctantly agreed with my decision to move off campus, though they insisted we live in a house with two bedrooms. If it made them feel better, I was okay with maintaining the illusion. My mother had come down once on a rare day off from the restaurant, bringing Frankie with her, and together, they helped me with some decorating.

Tonight, all of our friends had gathered to help us celebrate. Jeff was manning the make-your-own sundae station with Jesse's help, and Amanda and Jules were putting out the cookies and brownies on the table in the back. Even my brother Carl and Angela had driven up for the day, bringing Ma's cookies and one of Vince's famous rum cakes. But right now, the most important celebration was going on right here in the kitchen.

"We haven't properly broken in this counter top yet." Liam pulled me to the edge and ran his hands up my thighs.

"And we're not going to. Not right now, with everyone right outside the very thin walls." I pulled his face up to kiss his mouth, letting my tongue wander in teasing circles on the inside of his mouth.

He groaned into my mouth but eased back a little. "Then I guess I'll give you your housewarming present."

I rolled my eyes. "You don't buy me a housewarming gift, silly. You're moving in with me."

"Then just call it a surprise." He reached into the drawer to his left and pulled out some kind of remote control. His thumb moved over a button, and the entire house was flooded with music.

"You put in a sound system?" I held his face and kissed him, hard. "I love it. When did you do it?"

"Last week, while you were at the agency. Drew, that cop down the block, he helped me."

I smiled as Sinatra crooned about the way I looked tonight. Liam skimmed his fingers over my knees, teasing between my thighs. "Does this make you want to have a quickie right here, right now?" I laughed. "I want, yes. Not now. But later. Definitely later."

"Is that a promise?" He moved his lips down my neck, over to my ear, whispering until I shivered.

"Oh, yes. I promise."

Acknowledgments

Writing Ava and Liam's story was scary, even after so many wonderful bloggers and reviewers told me that they couldn't wait to read this book. I wasn't sure Liam was redeemable, but dang if he didn't prove me wrong.

Thanks to my fantabulous team at PBT and Hayson for helping me with every little thing. Mandie and Amanda, you keep me going when I swear I can't, and I love you both for it. Stacey and Jen, thank you for your support every day! All the PBT bloggers ...I always tell people you're the best in the business. It's the truth.

Stephanie Nelson came through once again with another amazing cover, and Stacey Blake made my pages so pretty. Amanda, your editing makes me laugh and keeps me on the straight and narrow. Thank you all!

My lovelies at Romantic Edge Books challenge me to be better, to strive harder and reach for the stars. I love you, ladies!

Olivia, thank you for being there for me no matter what, no matter when. So proud to be your friend!

My family has by now gotten used to the craziness of a writing mama. I get a little snarly at the end, but still ...it seems they still like me. Thanks especially to my daughter Haley and my son David who have stepped up to help me have more writing time. David, you are my number one assistant at events, too ...proud of you, always!

To my readers ...each message, each post, each review makes me smile. You truly make my world go round. Thank you for sticking by me. Rum cake and limoncello all around!

Ab♥ut the Auth♥r

Photo: Marilyn Bellinger

Tawdra Thompson Kandle lives in central Florida with her husband, children, cats and dog. She loves homeschooling, cooking, traveling and reading, not necessarily in that order. And yes, she has purple hair.

You can follow Tawdra here …

Facebook:
https://www.facebook.com/AuthorTawdraKandle

Twitter:https://twitter.com/tawdra

Website: tawdrakandle.com

Other Books by the Author

The King Series
Fearless
Breathless
Restless
Endless

The Posse

The Perfect Dish Duo
Best Served Cold

The Serendipity Duet
Undeniable
Unquenchable

ROMANTIC EDGE BOOKS

Meet the authors of Romantic Edge Books:
Eight Authors Writing Romance with an Edge

If you have enjoyed Just Desserts by Tawdra Kandle,
here are some other authors you may enjoy:

Oliva Hardin

Liz Schulte

C.G. Powell

Stephanie Nelson

Melissa Lummis

Tawdra Kandle

Other Books from Hayson Publishing

Through the Valley Love Endures by Eddie David Santiago

All for Hope by Olivia Hardin

The King Series by Tawdra Kandle

Fearless

Breathless

Restless

Endless

The Posse by Tawdra Kandle

Best Served Cold by Tawdra Kandle

Undeniable by Tawdra Kandle

Unquenchable by Tawdra Kandle

Imperfection by Phaedra Seabolt

Annie Crow Knoll: Sunrise by Gail Priest

Tough Love by Marcie A. Bridges

Haunted U by Jessica Gibson

Printed in the USA
CPSIA information can be obtained
at www.ICGtesting.com
JSHW031712140824
68134JS00038B/3649

9 781682 302552